Wisty & Judy
Thanks for all your great community involvement!
Robert ___
8/20/18

"In this free country, every man is at liberty to publish his own thoughts and impressions, and any witness who may differ from me should publish his own version of facts in the truthful narrative of which he is interested. I am publishing my own memoirs, not theirs, and we all know that no three honest witnesses of a simple brawl can agree on all the details."

William T. Sherman, Preface to the memoirs of General W.T. Sherman, Second Edition, Revised and Corrected, 1889

Cover photo: J. Robert Oppenheimer by Marie Hanson, Time Life Pictures/Getty Images

D1366534

Contents

Introduction

Three men walk into a bar, and a brawl ensues.

Everything that happens after that becomes the History of the brawl. There is little agreement about who threw the first punch, or why.

Six months later, no one remembers the details of the brawl—except that one man was killed.

A year later, three men walk into a bar, and a brawl ensues.

We have been taught that History is a chronological narrative of reasonably certain facts. In reality, the "facts" are often not certain and every event has multiple explanations—depending on who is telling the history.

The retelling of the bar brawl History, over time, increasingly infuses a blend of fact and fiction. We each embrace one "Real History" of the brawl in the bar as our official version of what transpired. The version we accept is usually the most compatible and comfortable with our values and world view.

We know that many events happening today have already happened— many times over. The short scenes in this book are "inspired by real events." What I am doing to History is similar to what Andy Warhol did to the Campbell soup can: put into a new context, what looks exactly like a soup can is transformed into art.

In these histories:
- an Irish immigrant runs for Congress from a jail cell
- a wealthy car manufacturer rents an ocean liner to seek world peace
- a Civil War General lectures on blackberries to avoid his own brutality
- a racist Congressman from Mississippi blocks legislation to make lynching a special crime

- an avowed Socialist seeks the Presidency from a federal penitentiary.
- a President admits his desire to crush his opponent
- a Congressman opposes a ban on assault weapons right after a school shooting
- an atomic scientist accused being a communist loses his life's work
- the King of Rock 'N Roll gets a narcotics agent badge
- a Naval Officer explains how to turn the Yellow race into loyal Americans
- a former Governor in a wool suit is questioned about homosexuality, and
- a gay psychiatrist disguises himself as Richard Nixon.

There are many ravings by Americans in these pages—wild talk about issues in the headlines today: racism, gun control, immigration, trade tariffs, sedition, gay rights, sexual affairs, civil rights, and the Cold War.

The wild talk is true history. Only the picture frames around the soup can have been changed.

And three men keep walking into a bar.

Albert Norman

HENRY'S SHIP OF FOOLS

Henry Ford walked down the steps of the Biltmore Hotel in New York City on the morning of December 4, 1915. He had chosen a long business coat with a fur collar, and his black bowler hat. He climbed into a Model T heading for Hoboken, New Jersey, where he would board the ocean liner Oscar II. His wife Clara, and son Edsel were by his side.

At Hoboken dockside, despite the cold December weather, Ford stopped to chat with the horde of reporters gathered by the ship, among a crowd estimated at roughly 15,000. He kissed his wife and son goodbye, exchanged words and an extended handshake with Thomas Edison, and some of his entourage. Ford was then lifted up onto the ship on a cargo platform, with the ship's captain and a dozen delegates surrounding him. They rose onto the long steamer, which had two huge white crosses painted on its hull, to remind submariner skippers of the ship's mission for peace. Ford was posing by the deck railing, waving to well-wishers on shore, when he reached into his coat pocket, and realized he had no passport. His staff on shore located the document and rushed it up to Ford.

In the last moments before departure, Thomas Edison, an old friend of Ford's, came onboard and weaved his way through the passengers to wish his friend luck. Photographers gathered to take images of Edison, in his black bow tie and long coat, posing with his right arm draped over Ford's shoulder. Ford turned to him and quietly said: "I'll give you a million dollars to come with us." Edison looked back at him, just smiled, shook his head, and took leave of the ship.

Propellers began to spin, black smoke was belching from the Oscar's single stack. The cheering from the crowd on the dock grew louder, and Ford, surrounded by peace delegates and his staff, waved to the crowd, his eyes searching for a last look at Clara and Edsel, who had apparently already motored away.

A prankster managed to toss a cage with two squirrels onto the deck of the Oscar II, with a note attached: "Live happy among the 'nuts.'"

Two hours after the Oscar II had left port, Ford asked the ship's crew to assemble passengers in the main ballroom, where he wished to give a welcoming address. Ford was dressed informally, with his shirt collar open. He had a small table beside him, and a glass of water with a carafe on it. There were roughly 44 reporters in the audience, along with 55 delegates to the peace conference, and another 56 students and members of Ford's staff. He spoke without notes.

"Friends, and fellow peace activists," he began. "Welcome aboard this Peace Ship. I am deeply grateful that you have joined us on this voyage. I want to share with you how we got to this place, at this time in history."

"Let me first share with you the news that Jane Addams, whom you all know, is bedridden in a hospital in Chicago with a serious kidney infection. Were this not so, I assure you that this leader of the peace movement, and the founder of Hull House, would be on this ship today!"

"I had a visit in November at my Dearborn home, Ten Eyck House from Rosika Schwimmer, who is my expert advisor, and Louis Lochner, my general secretary. Rosika, as you know, is an acclaimed pacifist and feminist, and Louis is the Secretary of the International Federation of Students. Without these two advisors, we would not be here on this Peace Ship steaming towards Norway, in pursuit of world peace."

"Last August, I pledged my fortune to achieving peace in Europe. Rosika wrote to me, asking for an interview. When Rosika and Louis came to my home, Madame Schwimmer went off with my wife into the gardens to 'talk things over,' as they said. Rosika won over Clara. She suggested to my wife that she should underwrite a telegram campaign to the White House for a neutral commission."

"Louis meanwhile briefed me on the content of his recent meeting with President Wilson. Louis felt we could show Wilson that the public wants peace. He said the President might call his own conference in Washington, and invite neutral nations to come, and to appoint a commission to this end. I told Louis, 'Whatever we decide to do, New York is the place for starting it.' I told him, 'I prefer men sitting around a table, not men dying in a trench.'"

When we all reconvened, Rosika made a passionate appeal for continuous mediation. I asked Louis what he thought of this plan: Was it practical? How much would it cost to maintain a neutral Commission? Louis and Rosika were in agreement that continuous mediation was the way to proceed. They suggested that I should tell Wilson that I would fund an official commission abroad and seek appropriations from Congress for it. I should tell the President that if we cannot operate through the White House, I would pursue peace independently, and unofficially. I then turned to Rosika, and I told her: 'Well, let's start. What do you want me to do?'"

"We shifted our operations to New York. When got to the Biltmore Hotel, I met with Jane Addams, Dean Kirchway of Columbia University, and others, and we all agreed that we needed to set up an official mediation commission to Europe. If the President agreed, it would have official status. If not, we would form our own private group."

Ford paused here to take a drink from the glass of water on the table.

"Lochner said—I think in a joking way—'Why not send a special ship to take delegates over?' I took to the idea immediately! A ship would give us great visibility. So, I looked into the cost of chartering a vessel, and asked Rosika to set up the details."

"The next day I went to Washington and had my meeting with the President. Louis was with me. To break the ice, I asked the President how he managed to look so fit. He said he had learned to leave his problems behind at the office. Then I told him one of my 'Ford Jokes:'

> I was driving by a cemetery and I saw a gravedigger who was digging a huge hole. I asked him if he was planning to bury a whole family? He said, No, the grave was only for one person. Then why so big? I asked him. He said the deceased had stipulated in his will that he be buried in his Ford—because his Ford had pulled him out of every hole to date—and he was sure it would pull him out of this one too!

"Wilson liked the joke and told me one of his own. Then we got down to business. I asked the President to support our neutral commission—and I offered to pay for it. Wilson told me he liked the idea--but he didn't want to focus on just one project.

"So, I asked him to reconsider. I told him that I had chartered a steamship that he was welcome to use, and that I had called for a press conference the next morning to discuss what the President and I had discussed. 'If you feel you can't act," I told him, 'I will.' He looked taken aback. But he still wouldn't budge. As we were being escorted out of the White House, Wilson said: 'Be careful of that gravedigger joke, Henry. This steamboat trip could bury your whole family.' Once we were outside the building, I turned to Lochner and said: 'He's a small man.'

"The next day, I told reporters at the Biltmore that 'we were going to try to get the boys out of the trenches before Christmas. I've chartered a ship, and some of us are going to Europe. I'm going to assemble the biggest and most influential peace activists in the country.' And here you are on this grand ship today."

"One reporter asked me today if I was anti-preparedness. Here's what I told him: "What could be more absurd and inconsistent than for us to ask Europe to stop adding to her own military burdens, while supporting either actively or passively a proposed increase of them in our own country?"

The audience burst into a round of applause that echoed off the steel walls of the banquet room. Ford used the break to take another sip of water.

"And the last thing I told reporters as I was boarding on this raw and bitter day, was: 'Tell the people to cry peace, and fight preparedness.' They asked me: 'What will you do if the expedition fails?' And I replied: 'I'll start another.'"

"I told my wife as we were parting: 'We've got peace-talk going now, and I'll pound it to the end.'"

Three days out at sea, a message was transmitted to the ship that President Wilson had asked Congress to increase funding for the army and the navy in the eventuality that the U.S. would be entering the war. The news circulated like an electric shock through the delegates, as dismay and disappointment spread.

The disheartening bulletin prompted a variety of responses. Some of the activists wanted to quickly draft a resolution to Congress rejecting Wilson's move towards war. Others were fearful of opposing Wilson, since he had stopped short of declaring war. Open quarrels broke out among the factions. Ford retreated to his cabin and was rarely seen on deck after that.

Below ship, in a small stateroom, Rosika Schwimmer and Louis Lochner sought to map out a response to Wilson's dramatic announcement. Schwimmer laid her large brim hat on the bed, and Lochner, still in his suit, removed his stiff collar.

"A few weeks ago," Schwimmer began, "if you had asked me, I would have told you I was living in Fairy-land...All I had to do was wave my wand for what I thought was needed for this Peace Mission, and lo! It appeared. But now...."

"We have a double-problem staring at us," Lochner said. "We have a back-sliding President inching towards war, and Ford himself is growing increasingly distant. He has been locked up in his cabin and is not responding to my repeated requests for an audience. His staff says he is ill from a cold---but I feel it is a deeper illness of disaffection. We are losing him."

"I think he has internalized this 'Ship of Fools' nonsense that our reporter friends are writing back home on a daily basis," Schwimmer said. "They are portraying us all as lunatics on the open sea."

"Their editors are hungry for war," Lochner replied. "The fighting that has broken out among pacifists on this ship is our own form of war—it will separate brother from brother."

"I saw the same thing happen while I was living in London," Schwimmer said, "when Britain entered the war. It was chaos in the peace movement. I came to the U.S. to meet with Wilson and William Jennings Bryan. I urged them both to convene a United States-sponsored neutral mediation conference. You see what a failure that effort was. And now we are at sea heading back to Europe."

"Some of our delegates have complained to me that you are stubborn and uncompromising. I am telling you only what I hear..." Lochner said.

"I have focused only on the ultimate goal of ending the war." Schwimmer said, raising her voice in anger. "Am I supposed to show patience for those who waiver from that goal?"

"Rosika---"

"Louis, you know that I have no sense of nationalism, only a cosmic consciousness of belonging to the human family. If brains have brought us to what we are in now, I think it is time to allow our hearts to speak. Our sons are being killed by the millions. We try to do good by going to the Presidents and Kings and Emperors. The only danger we face is a refusal."

"And it looks like we are in the teeth of another refusal now," Lochner added. "I am stunned by the foolish actions of Woodrow Wilson."

"Ford spoke the truth when he said Wilson was a small man. Our human rights are threatened by the ever-present spectre of war so destructive now of human material and moral values, as to render victory indistinguishable from defeat."

"But what do we do now with Ford?" Lochner asked. "He has become unreachable."

"We will go on to Norway, as planned." Rosika answered. "We have gotten this far. The only 'fools' on this ship are those who abandon the cause. We are looking into the mouth of a brutal war. Thousands—maybe millions of America's sons will die. If Mr. Ford has grown tired or weak, or perhaps even a deeper unhinging, it must make us even stronger and more determined to reach out to the neutral nations to prevent utter madness."

The two paused. Rosika picked up her hat and walked to the door. She turned and faced Lochner.

"Wilson has torn us apart, I don't want to let Ford do the same thing." And then as her hand turned the knob on the door she said:

"Henry has no love for Hungarian Jews. That much I have learned."

When the Oscar II arrived in Christiania, Norway, Ford was hustled off the ship to his own apartment, under the care of Clara's bodyguard. From his small lodging room, Ford sent a cable to his wife:

"Dearest Mother,

Our glorious mission has dissolved into bickering and petty factions. One day walking on deck I was hit by a wave and caught a bad cold. With that excuse, I have remained secluded in my cabin for days. But I assure you, I am on the mend.

Despite your fears that the Oscar II would be torpedoed in these submarine-infested waters, and that Edsel would be left an orphan, it was no German submarine that sank our ship. Our journey has been blown apart by our own internal confusion.

I am tired. I feel defeated. My spirits are low, and I have become depressed by the plots and counterplots swirling around me. I dare not venture out of my cabin lest I get caught up in this maelstrom. If you have been reading the press, you know that they say many of our activists are 'deluded.' Maybe the reporters were right: maybe this *was* a ship of deluded fools.

I told Lochner that I promised you, Clara, that I'd be back soon, 'Louis, you got this thing started,' I told him, 'and you can get along without me.' But I am most troubled over what I have heard about Schwimmer. It has been disconcerting. She has created more churning than the mighty Atlantic we have just crossed. Clara, it was you who first warned me about Schwimmer when she came to Ten Eyck. I believe in my heart that the Jews have caused the war. The Jews have caused the outbreak of thieving and robbery all over the country. I fear there is a vast Jewish conspiracy that is infecting America. The International Jew is leading us over the abyss, and I fear that in this ill-fated voyage I have just left, I have been the willing instrument of this Jewish conspiracy. I say with great regret and anguish, no good has come of this trip.

The good news, in short, is that I've decided to come home to Mother. Please forgive me for being led astray by my passions. I must find my own way home now.

With much love to you and Edsel,

Henry."

On Dec. 23rd at 4 am, 19 days after leaving America, Henry Ford slipped out of his hotel to board a ship back to New York. He abandoned the Ship of Fools.

Post Script

The delegates for the peace expedition traveled on to Norway, meeting with fellow pacifists in Sweden and Holland. In February, 1916, members of the neutral nations from Europe met with the Ford party in Stockholm, Sweden, to form the Neutral Conference for Continuous Mediation. The expedition returned from Europe in February of 1916. Work within the Neutral Conference for Continuous Mediation continued until the end of that year.

While living in the United States, Rosika Schwimmer was accused of being a German spy, and of being a Russian sympathizer. She attempted to become an American citizen, and sued the state of Illinois, which had rejected her application because she refused to swear to "take up arms" to defend America. Her case went to U.S. Supreme Court, which upheld the Illinois decision, but her denial of citizenship was reversed 17 years later by the Supreme Court.

Schwimmer received the World Peace Prize in 1937 and a decade later was nominated for the Nobel Peace Prize. She died in New York City at the age of 71.

Eight years after the Ship of Fools, Louis Lochner was hired to run the Associated Press' Berlin bureau, where he interviewed Adolf Hitler. He won a Pulitzer Prize for his articles written inside Germany during the war. Lochner was imprisoned by the Nazis, and after five months, was released as part of a prisoner swap. After the war, Lochner edited a book on the diary of Joseph Goebbels, Hitler's Chief of Propaganda. Lochner died in West Germany in 1975, at the age of 88.

During World War II, Henry Ford build a huge defense factory at Willow Run, near Detroit, which mass-produced the B-24 Liberator heavy bomber. When his son Edsel died in 1943, a frail Henry Ford was kept on as President of his company, but directors grew increasingly concerned over the auto company's financial decline. Ford eventually turned his company over to his grandson, Henry Ford II. Henry Ford died two years later at the age of 83.

DOCTOR HENRY ANONYMOUS

"I can't wear this mask," John Fryer insisted, looking into the brightly lit mirror of his hotel room in Dallas, Texas. "This wig looks like an old fish net."

"The whole image-thing just doesn't work. I'm a psychiatrist, not a freak. This Nixon mask just does-not-work. It's too sociopathic looking."

Fryer tried to center the rubber mask on his face, to make the eye holes match up with his. He tried pulling it higher up on head to make the hair look better. But nothing seemed to work.

"It makes the content of my speech seem like a joke." He looked again into the mirror for a few seconds, frowning underneath the mask. "It's hard to believe that under this get-up there's a farm boy from Winchester, Kentucky."

He walked out into the middle of the hotel room and held out his arms like he was surveying a large stage. "And listen to how this makes my voice sound. It's like I'm speaking inside a cave!"

Fryer lifted off the rubber mask, wiped his face with his hands, and put his reading glasses back on. He was wearing a bright red Hawaiian shirt with large yellow hibiscus flowers.

"John, don't go by the voice," said Barbara Gittings, the gay rights activist who had convinced Dr. Fryer to speak at the 1972 convention of the American Psychiatric Association. The world of psychiatry treated homosexuality as a disease. Barbara Gittings and Dr. John Fryer were determined to strike homosexuality from the Diagnostic and Statistical Manual of Mental Disorders, the psychiatrist's Bible.

Gittings was sitting at the small writing desk in the hotel room, scratching out some notes for her presentation on the panel with Fryer, and Harvard astronomer Frank Kameny, who had been fired from a federal job because of his homosexuality.

"You're going to be speaking through a microphone that will synthesize your voice anyway. It will totally distort it. The sound you're hearing now is not at all what your colleagues in the audience will hear."

"Barbara, we've got to alter this mask, somehow," Fryer suggested. "Can we cut it up, or twist it up in some way? I don't want people to associate homosexuality with Richard Nixon."

"Agreed. That would be an insult to gay people everywhere," Gittings said. "We've got time to work on the mask before you speak tomorrow. The point is: no one in the room will have any idea who you are. Just the fact that you are disguised will make the point. We want to dramatize the fact that you have to hide your identity to protect your job."

"I understand the guerilla theater aspect," Fryer said. "I just don't want to come on like some carnival show freak. I've been on the medical faculty of Temple University for 5 years. I want to get some respect here," he joked.

"Look, this whole convention is a freak show," Gittings said, rising from her chair and pacing by the window drapes. "Think about your appearance as a form of shock therapy to the psychiatric world. You're showing them that openly gay psychiatrists can lose their medical license! Let's remember the real freak show is out in the audience, where dozens of psychiatrists are desperately hoping their true sexuality won't be discovered. These are the folks who brought us chemical castration, electric shock therapy, and lobotomy. We're trying to convince these people to stop calling homosexuality a disease!"

Fryer walked over to the bed and picked up the suit coat of the tuxedo that was lying there, holding it up to the light. "It's funny," he recalled. "When I lost my job at Friends Hospital, the Administrator said to me: 'If you were gay and not flamboyant, we would keep you. If you were flamboyant and not gay we would keep you. But since you are both gay and flamboyant, we cannot keep you.' What would he say about my performance tomorrow?"

"Are you OK with the tux, the big bowtie and the ruffled shirt?" Gittings asked.

"Well, the tux fits like I'm wearing a tent," Fryer laughed. I'm a pretty large guy—but that tuxedo looks like it was fitted for a sumo wrestler on a camping expedition."

"We agreed to find an 'oversized' tuxedo---that's what you've got."

"Nixon would never be caught dead in this tuxedo," Fryer quipped.

"Nixon would never be caught dead with a 35 year old gay psychiatrist," Gittings shot back.

"And thank God for that," Fryer said.

He sat on the bed and tried on the pants from the tux suit, pulling each leg over his large shoes. The fit was baggy---but not too exaggerated.

"I look like 'Bozo-does-Dallas!'" he grumbled.

"Do you want to rehearse some pieces from the speech?" Gittings asked.

"Sure, and then we can do dinner in the hotel restaurant."

"Go, ahead. I'll listen as if I were a straight shrink," Gittings laughed.

"OK, this is Take One of the panel called *Psychiatry: Friend or Foe to Homosexuals: A Dialogue.* Fryer cleared his throat and held out his script so he could he easily read the large font.

"I start off by thanking Dr. Robinson," Fryer said, "then I get right into it."

"I am a homosexual. I am a psychiatrist." Fryer read. "I, like most of you in this room, am a member of the APA and am proud to be a member. However, tonight I am, insofar as it is possible, a 'we.' I attempt tonight to speak for many of my fellow gay members of the APA as well as for myself...Several of us feel that it is time that real flesh and blood stand up before you and ask to be listened to and understood insofar as that is possible. I am disguised tonight in order that I might speak freely without conjuring up too much regard on your part about the particular WHO I happen to be. I do that mostly for your protection. I can assure you that I could be any one of more than a hundred psychiatrists registered at this convention. And the curious among you should cease attempting to figure out who I am, and listen to what I say..."

Fryer paused and said as an aside: "I don't think I should say anything here about my not having tenure. What do you think, Barbara?"

"I like it so far. I would leave out the 'tenure issue' for now. We can always go back and edit it in."

"OK, so I continue: "We homosexual psychiatrists must persistently deal with a variety of what we shall call 'Nigger Syndromes.' We shall describe some of them and how they make us feel."

"As psychiatrists who are homosexual, we must know our place and what we must do to be successful. If our goal is academic appointment, a level of earning capacity equal to our fellows, or admission to a psychoanalytic institute, we must make certain that no one in a position of power is aware of our sexual orientation or gender identity."

"Much like the black man with the light skin who chooses to live as a white man, we cannot be seen with our real friends---our real homosexual family---lest our secret be known and our dooms sealed. There are practicing psychoanalysts among us who have completed their training analysis without mentioning their homosexuality to their analysts. Those who are willing to speak up openly will do so only if they have nothing to lose, then they won't be listened to."

Fryer looked over at Gittings. "Is that 'Nigger Syndrome' thing too much?"

"I don't think so," Gittins said. "It may shock or offend some people—but that's what we're doing anyway, right?"

"As psychiatrists who are homosexuals," Fryer continued, "we must look carefully at the power which lies in our hands to define the health of others around us. In particular, we should have clearly in our minds, our own particular understanding of what it is to be a healthy homosexual in a world, which sees that appellation as an impossible oxymoron. One cannot be healthy and be homosexual, they say."

"Will people follow that?" Fryer asked.

"No one in the audience will know what a 'healthy homosexual' is," Gittings replied. "Little warning alarms will be going off in hundreds of over-educated brains."

"I am an exhibit of a healthy homosexual," Fryer said, and picked up his speech again:

"One result of being psychiatrists who are homosexual is that we are required to be more healthy than our heterosexual counterparts. We have to make some sort of attempt through therapy or analysis to work problems out. Many of us who make that effort are still left with a sense of failure and of persistence of 'the problem.'"

"Just as the black man must be a super person, so must we, in order to face those among our colleagues who know we are gay. We could continue to cite examples of this sort of situation for the remainder of the night. It would be useful, however, if we could now look at the reverse."

Fryer stopped to pencil in a notation in the margin: "Edit the piece about 'more healthy?'"

"What is it like to be a homosexual who is also a psychiatrist?" he continued. "Most of us gay psychiatrists do not wear our badges into the Bayou Landing," ("That's a gay bar in Dallas," Fryer noted) "or the local Canal Baths. If we did, we could risk the derision of all the non-psychiatrist homosexuals. There is much negative feeling in the homosexual community towards psychiatrists. And those of us who are visible are the easiest targets from which the angry can vent their wrath. Beyond that, in our own hometowns, the chances are that in any gathering of homosexuals, there is likely to be any number of patients or paraprofessional employees who might try to hurt us professionally in a larger community if those communities enable them to hurt us that way."

"I would leave out the 'bar and Canal Bath' references," Gittings suggested. "I don't think you need it."

"Finally," Fryer continued, "as homosexual psychiatrists, we seem to present a unique ability to marry ourselves to institutions rather than wives or lovers. Many of us work 20 hours daily to protect institutions that would literally chew us up and spit us out if they knew the truth. These are our feelings, and like any set of feelings, they have value insofar as they move us toward concrete action."

"OK, now I do a little shift here—I may want to do some edits." Fryer said.

"I will speak primarily to the other members of the gay psychiatrist community who are present--not in costume--tonight. Perhaps you can help your fellow psychiatrist friends understand what I am saying. When you are with professionals, fellow professionals, fellow psychiatrists who are denigrating the 'faggots' and the 'queers,' don't just stand back, but don't give up your careers, either. Show a little creative ingenuity; make sure you let your associates know that they have a few issues that they have to think through again. When fellow homosexuals come to you for treatment, don't let your own problems get in your way, but develop creative ways to let the patient know that they're all right. And teach them everything they need to know. Refer them to other sources of information with basic differences from your own so that the homosexual will be freely able to make his own choices."

"Good," Gittings smiled.

"Finally, pull up your courage by your bootstraps, and discover ways in which you and homosexual psychiatrists can be closely involved in movements which attempt to change the attitudes of heterosexuals--and homosexuals---toward homosexuality. For all of us have something to lose. We may not be considered for that professorship. The analyst down the street may stop referring us his overflow. Our supervisor may ask us to take a leave of absence."

18

"That shit actually happened to me," Fryer said. "Tenure is just a form of prolonged academic terrorism."

"We are taking an even bigger risk however," he went on, " not accepting fully our own humanity, with all of the lessons it has to teach all the other humans around us and ourselves. This is the greatest loss: our honest humanity. And that loss leads all those others around us to lose that little bit of their humanity as well. For, if they were truly comfortable with their own homosexuality, then they could be comfortable with ours. We must use our skills and wisdom to help them---and us---grow to be comfortable with that little piece of humanity called homosexuality."

Fryer ended. He walked over to the small writing table, put down his speech carefully, and placed his pencil on top of the papers. He turned around and faced Gittings, with his hands in his pockets, his head tilted slightly as if to hear her fully.

"Well?" he said. "What do the critics say, Barbara? Please don't hold back...."

After a short pause, Gittings smiled broadly and said: "I think its brilliant, John. This is going to really shake up psychiatry. You are the right person to say these things, and at the right time. I'm just feeling very grateful that you agreed to do this panel. Thank you so much, John. Even in disguise, this is a very, very brave thing to do."

"You've brought me this far, Barbara! I didn't accept your invitation right away," Fryer reminded her. "I had to think about it a lot. It seemed like something that had to be done. I was thrown out of a residency because I was gay. I lost a job because I was gay...This had to be said. I just can't do it as me yet. Someday, I hope to be tenured---and tenured by a chairman who knows I am gay. Then I won't need a mask and a wig."

The two friends just looked at each other, as the Dallas evening washed out the light from the windows.

Fryer sat down in the small chair by the writing desk. His right hand was cupped over his chin and mouth. He closed his eyes.

"I don't know if any of this brings about change," Fryer said, mostly to himself. "I'm comfortable trying to change one person at a time. But I don't know about this circus tomorrow..."

Gittings sat opposite Fryer, not certain if he wanted an answer from her or not.

Taking off his glasses, Fryer rubbed his eyes, and held his glasses up the overhead light. He casually tossed the Nixon mask onto the hotel bed.

"What if," he sighed, "what if my colleagues remember me only as 'That faggot in the Nixon mask?' What if they run into me on the streets of Philadelphia two years from now, and say: 'Hey, weren't you that queer in the Nixon mask?'

What am I supposed to say back? "Yeah, I was that queer?""

Post Script:

Twenty-two years after his speech before the American Psychiatric Association, Fryer revealed at an APA Convention that he was Dr. Henry Anonymous. The APA did remove homosexuality from the Diagnostic and Statistical Manual one year after Fryer's speech. But for years afterwards, the debate over homosexuality as a mental disorder continued.

Fryer was appointed a professor at Temple University. He specialized in the treatment of drug and alcohol addiction, and death and bereavement. He treated gay men with AIDS as part of his private practice. He died in 2003 at the age of 64.

Barbara Gittings worked for a decade and a half to introduce positive materials about gays into American libraries, and to end job discrimination against homosexuals. She helped create the National Gay and Lesbian Task Force. In 1999, Gittings was honored for a lifetime of contributions to the LGBT movement by PrideFest, who called her "the Rosa Parks of the gay and lesbian civil rights movement." She died in Pennsylvania in 2007 at the age of 74.

SUNBURNT YANKEES

In January of 1922, the U.S. House of Representatives voted to adopt an anti-lynching bill, which had been introduced by a legislator from Missouri four years earlier. The bill, which sought to punish lynching and other forms of mob violence, was reintroduced several times in Congress, but each time was blocked by Southern lawmakers in the Senate who filibustered against the bill. The anti-lynching bill became a symbol of the still tender wound that existed between the North and the South, some 60 sixty years after the conclusion of the Civil War.

The anti-lynching bill, which had the support of Republican President Warren Harding, classified lynching as a federal felony, which gave the federal government the right to prosecute cases. Congress felt that state and local jurisdictions had done an inadequate job in pursuing such cases.

Under the anti-lynching bill, a state or local official who failed to protect a person from lynching could face up to 5 years in jail and a $5,000 fine. Anyone who took part in a lynching would receive at least 5 years in prison. Any county in which a lynching took place would be subject to a $10,000 fine, which would be paid to the victim's family or his parents. If the victim of a lynching was seized in one county and killed in another---both counties would pay the fine.

Congressman John Elliott Rankin of Mississippi was a vocal opponent of the anti-lynching bill. When he was invited to speak by the Masons in Tupelo, he saw it as a fresh opportunity to state his case before his constituents, confident that the overwhelming sentiment in his District was against the anti-lynching bill. As a Congressman facing re-election every two years, these kinds of emblematic issues were an invaluable context for a stump speech.

When he entered the Masonic Hall, it was through the rear entrance. The meeting was already underway. Rankin took a seat quietly at the back of the room, as the master of ceremonies gaveled the meeting to order.

"Brothers, our speaker this afternoon is someone that Members of the Tupelo Masonic Lodge 318 know well. Representative John Elliott Rankin is a proud son of Itawamba County, and a graduate of the University of Mississippi law school. He is a life-long Democrat, and he knows the people of this state better than anyone I know. That's why the voters of Mississippi sent him to represent us in Congress two years ago—and in that time Mr. Rankin has shown us that our confidence in him was well-placed. We have invited Congressman Rankin to join our Brethren today to apprise us of what has been going on in Washington, D.C. that might affect his constituents back home in Tupelo and across Mississippi. Please welcome our distinguished Congressman, John Elliott Rankin."

The audience of around 80 Masons applauded Congressman Rankin as he weaved his steps through the banquet tables set with fried fish, corn bread, and pecan pie, to find his way to the head table. Rankin, who recently turned 40, was elected to Congress in 1920. The son of a Tupelo schoolteacher, Rankin's family had come from South Carolina 60 years ago.

After getting his law degree from the University of Mississippi, Rankin set up a practice in Clay County where he grew up. He and his wife, Annie Laurie Burrous, had a daughter, Annie Laurie Rankin. Rankin wore a close-fitted brown suit, with a high collar and knotted tie. He was considered to be 'more than fair handsome' in the opinion of his hometown admirers.

"Free and Accepted Masons," Rankin began, "Brethren, let me thank you for inviting me to share this fine lunch with you today. And thanks for that kind introduction from your Worshipful Master, R.L. Senter, who has served Lodge 318 so well since his election last year. R.L. has done an outstanding job of letting me know, as your Congressman, what is uppermost on the minds of the men of Mississippi. Thank you for that R.L!"

R.L. Senter rose briefly from his seat and waved in acknowledgement of the sustained applause that erupted at the mention of the Master's name.

"Now, I will assure you." Rankin continued, "that there has never been a more critical period in Congress for the good people of Mississippi. And I know that you want me to fill you in on the concerns you have expressed to me over the matter of this legislation that has come to be called the 'anti-lynching bill,' recently on the floor of the House."

Outside of the scattered clink of china tea cups and silverware on plates, the room grew quiet.

"This legislation, gentlemen, is one of the most drastic and most vicious measures that ever came before the House. If I thought it would stop lynchings, and at the same time prevent the awful causes of lynchings, I would consider giving it my support. But the fact is, this legislation infringes on the rights of the States, does violence to the Constitution, destroys the rights of our citizens, and unjustly penalizes innocent persons for the offenses of other people."

"This bill is but a play to the Negro agitator for political effect, and it will not only fail to decrease the number of lynchings, or remedy the causes thereof, but it will encourage the Negro brutes in their attacks on the defenseless white women of the Mississippi, and this great country."

The room broke into loud applause, with many members clinking their forks against their tea cups or water glasses.

"This legislation ought to be called 'A bill to encourage rape.' That will be the result if it becomes the law. It will cost the lives of innocent white women and children throughout the South, if not throughout the entire country."

"Men from the North have never known what it means to live in a state of constant dread for the safety of your loved ones. Heretofore they have had little or no race question. But in the South, it is different. The shadow of the Negro criminal constantly hangs like the sword of Damocles over the head of every white woman in the South, and no one knows just when or where it is going to fall."

"The vicious Negroes will understand from this bill that they are protected in their crimes. They will see that by its terms they are assured of the protection of the Federal Government, and that if their crimes are so revolting as to invoke the wrath of an outraged community to such an extent that they rise up and take the life of the offender, then that community or county is to be fined the sum of $10,000, to be paid to his family, no matter how atrocious his crime may have been."

Rankin paused his speech and looked out into the room. Cries of "blasphemy," and "lynch Congress" arose from the crowd.

"In other words," the Congressman continued, "this bill insures the life of the Negro rapist for $10,000, to be paid to his family by the family and the neighbors of his victim. Already this bill is producing results: four assaults were committed on white women by Negro brutes during the first week of its consideration by the House. One of them took place in an apartment house in the city of Washington, right in the very shadow of the dome of the Capitol. Another occurred in the State of Maryland less than 50 miles away. One occurred in Pittsburgh, Pennsylvania, and another in Hattiesburg, Mississippi. And how many others happened in other sections of the country, God only knows."

"As I have said, I am not in favor of lynching, and never have been. I wish it were in my power to forever stamp it out. But there is only one way in which that can be done, and that is to remove the cause, to stop the awful crimes for which men are thus put to death. For no matter what the law is, so long as those outrages continue, society will be occasionally shocked by outbreaks of mob violence. But this bill is not designed to prevent the cause of lynching, nor have its supporters uttered a single word against the commission of those horrible crimes of which lynchings are the logical results."

"Let me share this story: Several years ago, a Negro brute entered a home---not very far from where I live---in which there were only two persons at the time, a mother and her daughter. The mother knew the moment she looked upon his savage countenance what his hellish designs were. She rushed between him and his intended victim, met him at the door of her daughter's room, when he seized her, drew a razor, and cut her throat from ear to ear. She held the gaping wound with her hands and shrieked loud enough to warn her daughter to flee, and thereby saved her from a more terrible fate. When the men of that community gathered and looked upon that dead mother, who had laid down her life to save her daughter from this demon in human form, do you suppose they remained cool and collected and conducted themselves as rational men?"

"There has been something said in the course of this debate about the Negro that was put to death in Memphis, Tennessee two years ago. One morning the whole community was shocked by one of the most horrible crimes ever committed by a human being. A beautiful little girl about 13 or 14 years of age, who lived just on the outskirts of Memphis, was waylaid on her way to school by a Negro man who was more than 50 years old. He secluded himself at the only point on the road where this child had to pass out of sight of a dwelling house, and when she came along he seized her, dragged her into a secluded spot, outraged her, mutilated her little body beyond description, and then took his ax and chopped her head off, hid her head among some bushes, and then threw her little body into an old slough, and went on his way. When they captured him, he confessed to the crime and told his captors where to find the remains. Is it reasonable to suppose that those people would remain cool under those circumstances?"

"In one town in the District which I have the honor to represent, several years ago, a little woman was standing before the mirror combing her hair, when she saw in its reflection the countenance of a black demon approaching stealthily from the rear. She knew at once what he meant. She reached and got her husband's pistol, but she was too weak to pull the trigger hard enough to make it fire. He saw from her trembling hand that she could not defend herself, and he walked up, took the weapon from her hand, choked her to insensibility, outraged her, and then took a razor, cut her throat, and left her weltering in her own blood in the parlor of her own home. I wonder what would have happened if this had occurred in your community?"

"I relate these three instances, my friends, as illustrations of the conduct Congress is encouraging on the part of the criminal element of the Negro race by this iniquitous bill. You may say that these are isolated cases. But I can recall a large number of them that are just as revolting as these."

Rankin paused to let the murmurs in the room die down.

"A vast number of innocent white women are outraged by Negroes in the South every year, and now this evil is creeping into the North. Their time is coming; the Negroes are migrating to the North, and the day is not far distant when they will awake to a realization of the fact that they have a more serious race problem on their hands than the South has on hers."

Once again, the room was swollen with applause, with a few members rising to their feet to cheer on Congressman Rankin.

"This is an issue that is as old as man himself." Rankin said, lowering his voice. "Its history may be traced in the records of those nations whose monuments mark the path of time. For thousands of years it has in risen to vex the minds of statesmen and mar the progress of the human race. It is the evil genius of our civilization, the sprig of poison ivy in the laurel wreath that crowns America's wonderful achievements."

Rankin smiled inwardly as he recalled that it was one of his young legislative aides from Itawamba County who had first suggested the 'sprig of poison ivy in the laurel wreath' metaphor. Rankin didn't like the comparison at first--- but he used the phrase today as if it were a newly-cut turn of phrase he had just conjured up.

"It rent this Republic in civil feuds and drenched her soil in fraternal blood and has kept our people divided by partisan strife and sectional feelings for more than a hundred years. It constitutes the death's-head at the feast of international disarmament. Its sinister gaze is falling with slant-eyed racial envy upon the fairest portion of the Pacific coast, disturbing the tranquility of that great section, and has frightened the party in power into an almost ignominiously prodigal program of naval and military expenditures. It is an issue which will permit of only four possible solutions—amalgamation, extermination, deportation, and segregation."

"Let me explain, Tupelo Brothers, what these four propositions mean. We must inevitably resort to one of them to arrive at a Settlement. Which one shall it be?"

"Amalgamation means the intermarriage and intermixture of the two races. It is too repulsive even for consideration. God forbid that the line of cleavage between the white man and the Negro in this country should ever be broken down. If it should be, then America, once proud America, would soon find herself sinking hopelessly into the implacable mire of mongrelism. The Negro is not the equal of the White man, and he never will be. It is impossible to reverse the laws of nature and lift the Negro through tens of thousands of years of civilization, education, and development, regenerate him, purge him of his weaknesses and his instincts, and endow him with Caucasian strength, traits, and characteristics, and make him the peer of the white man."

"What has the Negro done for himself or for civilization to entitle him to equality with the white race? The only civilization he has ever imbibed was that imposed upon him by the White people of the South through the unfortunate institution of slavery—unfortunate for the white man; fortunate for the Negro. For tens of thousands of years, he roamed at will over the continent of Africa, the richest country of all the world, feasting upon his fellow man, and never even developed the art of agriculture to the extent of making his living out of the ground. For countless ages he trod the sands of his native soil with diamonds beneath his feet and never even dreamed of the theory of values."

"All the Negro ever learned was to construct a rude shelter of bark and grass sufficient to shield his head from the beating rays of a tropical sun. He remained in this savage state until he was brought to our shores and shown the light of civilization through the institution of slavery—the worst curse that ever befell the South, and the greatest blessing the Negro has ever known."

More applause and rattling of tea cups.

"Amalgamation is out of the question. For my part, I would rather know that our population would sink into the grave with the death of this generation, and that this continent would again become a howling wilderness, to be later settled up by the white races of other lands, than to see our people accept the Negroes on terms of social equality and our country go down to the future inhabited by a degraded mongrel race."

"The next possible solution is extermination, which is too horrible to contemplate. It will only be resorted to if the fanaticism--which this bill reflects--continues to fan the flame of race hatred until the two races are driven to open warfare. This agitation is not coming from the Negroes of the South. It is coming from the deluded Afro-Americans in and around

Washington, Chicago, St. Louis, Boston, and other places where a few misguided people have led them to believe that they are merely sunburnt Yankees and entitled to be placed on equality with the white man. If this feeling continues to grow, it will ultimately result in the extermination of the Negro race in America."

"The Negro will fill the northern cities, towns, and hamlets, until they will have a race problem compared with which ours in the South will shrink to insignificance. I predict that within less than 25 years from today, some of the very districts whose Representatives are behind this bill will be crying aloud for help to rid them of this Negro scourge, and possibly be answered only by the echo of their wailing cry."

"The third available solution is deportation, which is hardly feasible at this time--although it may be the ultimate solution. But it will be a long time, to say the least of it, before the people of this country, both white and black, will consent to a final separation. The question is before us now, and a solution less drastic must be found."

"The solution, my Brothers, is segregation. Segregation--or a separation of the races--is the only immediate reasonable, humane, sensible solution of this great question. We need to segregate the races not only socially, but politically as well. There ought to be a law in every State in the Union prohibiting intermarriage between the races, and they ought to be separated in all governmental activities: in the Army, in the Navy, in schools, and on street cars, railroad trains, and other common carriers. There ought to be, and there must be, before this question is settled, a segregation law in every State, separating whites. and Negroes in the residential sections of cities, towns, and municipalities."

More applause. Rankin asked for a glass of water, which a negro waiter in a starched white suit brought to him, with a wedge of lemon added.

"In the South we have done that. We are segregated by a common understanding. The Negro abides by it, for he knows it is best for himself as well as for the white man. In the North, they will be driven to this salutary recourse within the very near future, and the sooner you wake up and adopt it, the better it will be for all concerned."

"Brothers, I have no antipathy for the Negro as a race. I have no prejudice against him because he is a Negro. I am a far better friend to him than any man who votes for this bill. But I understand him. I know his weaknesses, his shortcomings, and his limitations. I want to see him protected in the enjoyment of life, liberty, and the pursuit of happiness. And in order to protect him in those enjoyments and save him from the disastrous consequences of further misunderstandings with the white people of this country, in order to protect the white people against the contamination of an inferior race, in order to perpetuate the glories of this great Republic and reunite her in the bonds of fraternal love and mutual understanding, in order that her blessings may be showered on the generations yet unborn, I have implored---on the very floor of the House of Representatives in Washington, D.C.---that the men of the North join with the men of the South in the only just and equitable solution of this great problem---a segregation of the two races."

The dining room seemed to vibrate from the strength of applause that lasted for a full minute. Rankin used a pocket handkerchief to wipe the corners of his mouth. He resettled his body and prepared to close his speech.

"I thank you, Brothers, for supporting me in my endeavors to explain the Southern Man to members of Congress. I know that's what you sent me to Washington to do, and I will protect and defend your honor and the honor of Mississippi always---you can count on that!"

"Let me remind you, Brothers, that I will soon be standing for re-election, and your generous financial support now will ensure that your voice on issues like this anti-lynching bill will sound like a clarion on Capitol Hill."

Everyone pushed back their chairs and rose to their feet. Worshipful Master R.L. Senter the asked the room to join him in singing a of the chorus of "The Bonnie Blue Flag:"

"We are a band of brothers

And native to the soil,

Fighting for the property

We gained by honest toil;

And when our rights were threatened,

The cry rose near and far—

'Hurrah for the Bonnie Blue Flag

That bears a single star!'

Hurrah! Hurrah!

For Southern rights hurrah!

Hurrah for the Bonnie Blue Flag

That bears a single star."

As Congressman Rankin was exiting the room, a small man in a white suit came up to him, and with this right hand jammed a $500 bill into Rankin's coat pocket. "That currency in your pocket has an engraving on the back of DeSoto discovering the Mississippi in 1541," the man said. "Use it towards your next election!"

"I thank you, sir, for that gesture," Rankin said, bowing slightly from the waist.

"Just one favor, Congressman," the man said, returning the bow. "Don't let that anti-lynching bill ever reach President Harding. I know that fool would put his name to it."

"Never fear," Rankin replied, "the Southern filibuster will hang that bill's chances---forever. Tell your wife and your daughters---if daughters you have—that they can rest easy on that promise tonight. We shall keep the Negroes from her door."

Postscript:

John Elliot Rankin served as a Congressman from Mississippi for 32 years. He remained a reliable vote for the segregation movement and white supremacy. While in Congress, he proposed a bill to outlaw interracial marriage, and opposed efforts to eliminate Mississippi's use of the poll tax, which kept poor people from voting.

From the floor of the House of Representatives, Rankin espoused broad racist views not only towards Blacks, but Japanese Americans as well as Jews. Rankin attacked Albert Einstein as a "foreign-born agitator" who sought "to further the spread of Communism throughout the world." Rankin once referred to the Jewish newspaper columnist Walter Winchell as "the little kike." Rankin endorsed an effort to keep Japanese and Negro blood donations during the war from being mixed with white blood.

In 1947, Rankin ran for a seat in the U.S. Senate representing Mississippi. He lost the race, securing only 13% of the votes cast. Five years later, when his district was combined with another district, Rankin lost his House seat to a Democratic challenger, and retired from politics.

Rankin died in Tupelo, Mississippi in 1960 at the age of 78. Congress never passed an anti-lynching bill.

PROVIDENTIAL BLACKBERRY

Two years after the opening of the Michigan Military Academy in Orchard Lake Village, William Tecumseh Sherman, General of the Army, accepted an invitation to speak to the graduating class. An estimated 10,000 people came to hear his speech on June 19,1879. The village had never experienced a crowd of such size.

The Civil War had ended only 14 years before Sherman traveled to the Academy to speak. His name had become synonymous with the concept of "total war" during his command of the Union armies of the West, as he led them from Chattanooga to Atlanta---the notorious "march to the sea" across Georgia—and then northward from Savannah through the Carolinas. Sherman was widely viewed as having dealt the death blow to the Confederacy. As such, he was feared and hated below the Mason-Dixon Line, and held in some suspicion by Northerners for the destruction he left behind in every city and town he conquered.

Sherman readily accepted the invitation from Captain J. Sumner Rogers to speak at the Academy. The General had a distinct fondness for military academies. He had graduated from West Point in 1840, and when the South seceded from the Union, Sherman was serving as the superintendent of a military college in Louisiana. At Captain Rogers' request, Sherman also agreed to speak privately with a smaller assembly of boys at the school's assembly hall after his public speech.

In that smaller, intimate session, Sherman sat on a wooden chair facing the graduates. He removed his broad yellow-colored sash which draped from his right shoulder across his chest and undid the rows of gold-colored buttons on his military jacket. The press often referred to him as the General "with the sandy-colored beard."

As in many such gatherings, the first question asked by a graduate was: "Where did you get your middle name?"

"I was born in Ohio, just a few years after the War of 1812," Sherman answered. "My father caught a fancy for the Shawnee Chief Tecumseh, who fought with the British, and who tried to unite Ohio River Valley Native American Tribes. I remember reading that Tecumseh said you should 'never let the fear of death enter your heart.' 'Trouble no one about their religion,' he said. 'Respect others in their view, and demand that they respect yours. Love your life. Perfect your life. Beautify all things in your life. Seek to make your life long and its purpose in the service of your people.' I think those are good enough words by which to live your life."

"Is it true, General, that you told General Grant that you 'could make Georgia howl?'. And did you say you would 'turn South Carolina into a wilderness?'" another graduate asked.

Sherman looked the boy straight in the eye, his right arm cocked on his knee. "When I arrived in Atlanta, I told the Mayor: 'If you and your citizens will give up, I and this army will become your greatest protectors.' By the time I got to Savannah, the city was completely subjugated. I saw no need to destroy the city's military and industrial facilities, or to destroy private homes. I issued a detailed order that allowed soldiers to gather food and forage liberally on the country---but prohibited them from trespassing or entering homes. As a Christmas gift, I gave President Lincoln the city of Savanna and its 25,000 bale of cotton."

Sherman stopped for a moment, and looked over at his host, Captain Rogers, to see if his plain manner of speaking had been too excessive for his young audience. But Rogers appeared smiling, and relaxed.

"My goal." Sherman continued, "was to make my adversaries so sick of war that generations would pass away before they would again appeal to it. And remember, I was stationed in Fort Moultrie in Charleston in the 1840s. I know the South and have a great affection for it---but I could not tolerate insults to our country or cause. When people speak contemptuously of the flag, which is the silent emblem of our country, I will not go out of my way to protect them or their property. If the people raised a howl against my barbarity and cruelty, I would answer that 'war is war, and not popularity-seeking.' If they wanted peace, they and their relatives needed to stop the war. We needed to make old and young, rich and poor, feel the hard hand of war."

Another graduate rose to his feet. "Did you regret, sir, the outbreak of war?"

"I knew as early as 1850 that our nation was on the eve of civil war. Southern politicians openly asserted as much. Mr. Seward had publicly declared that no government could possibly exist half slave and half free.

31

Yet our Government made no military preparations, and the Northern people generally paid no attention--took no warning of its coming and would not realize its existence until Fort Sumter was fired on by batteries of artillery, handled by declared enemies. The South understood that its chances of winning a war were yearly lessened by the fact that all the European immigrants were coming to the Northern States, and none to the Southern."

"The slave population in 1860 was near four million, and the money value thereof not far from twenty-five hundred million dollars. A cause that endangered so vast a moneyed interest was an adequate cause of anxiety and preparation. Northern leaders surely ought to have foreseen the danger and prepared for it. But they did not. After the election of Mr. Lincoln, there was no concealment of the declaration and preparation for war in the South. When war was actually begun, the North put out a call for 75,000 "ninety-day" men, because Mr. Seward believed that the war would be concluded in ninety days."

"But how did you manage to move so many men and material so quickly through the South," asked a boy who said he was from Nebraska.

"Traveling on the road, I estimated that we needed to have 5,000 men to a mile. A full corps of 30,000 men would extend six miles. Add in trains and batteries of artillery, and it would draw out to ten miles. On a long march, the leading division should be on the road by the earliest dawn, and march at the rate of about two and a half miles an hour, reaching camp by noon. The rear divisions and trains would not reach camp much before night. A brigade of 3,000 infantry would occupy a mile of 'front.' For a strong line of battle 5,000 men with two batteries should be allowed to each mile."

"Would you call that the calculus of war?" the boy followed up.

"On long marches," Sherman added, "the artillery and wagon-trains should always have the right of way. The troops should improvise roads to one side, and all trains should have escorts to protect them, and to assist them in bad places. Each soldier should---unless sick or wounded---carry his musket and equipment containing from 40 to 60 rounds of ammunition, his shelter-tent, a blanket or overcoat, and an extra pair of pants, socks, and drawers, in the form of a scarf, worn from the left shoulder to the right side in lieu of knapsack. In his haversack he should carry some bread, cooked meat, salt, and coffee. I do not believe a soldier should be loaded down too much, but, including his clothing, arms, and equipment, he can carry about 50 pounds without impairing his health or activity. By such a distribution a corps can thus carry the equivalent of 500 wagon-loads—which is an immense relief to the trains..."

A final question came from the rear of the hall from a graduate who said he was originally from Virginia.

"General, you have walked quite carefully around the issue of the brutality and the bestiality of combat—yet in your speech earlier today you warned us that 'war is hell.' Have you not, Sir---given all the death and destruction you have left in your wake---been responsible for creating much Hell on Earth? And have you, yourself, not become sick of war?"

Sherman's back muscles tensed underneath his uniform, and his jaw tightened down into a locked position. His dark eyes appeared aflame, and he pulled at his short-cropped beard. At this point Captain Rogers rose to his feet and lifted his arms as if to signal the end of the meeting. But Sherman rose also, and waved Rogers down.

"I note that the lunch hour is drawing near, and with it, thoughts of food," Sherman said calmly. "Although little has been written about this subject, let me assure you that the 'feeding' of an army is a matter of the most vital importance and demands the earliest attention of the general entrusted with a campaign. To be strong, healthy, and capable of the largest measure of physical effort, a soldier needs about 3 pounds gross of food per day, and his horse or mule about 20 pounds. When a general first estimates the quantity of food and forage needed for an army of 50,000 of 100,000 men, he is apt to be dismayed."

"A good General must give this subject his personal attention, for the army reposes in him alone. In my opinion, there is no better food for man than beef-cattle driven on the hoof, issued liberally, served with salt, bacon, and bread. Coffee has also become almost indispensable, though many substitutes were found for it, such as Indian-corn, roasted, ground, and boiled as coffee. The sweet-potato, and the seed of the okra plant are prepared in the same way. All these were used by the people of the South, who for years could procure no coffee---but I noticed that the women always begged of us some real coffee---which seems to satisfy a natural yearning or craving more powerful than can be accounted for on the theory of habit."

Wiping one hand across his mouth, Sherman continued. "I would advise that the coffee and sugar ration be carried along, even at the expense of bread, for which there are many substitutes. Of these, Indian-corn is the best and most abundant. Parched in a frying-pan, it is excellent food, or if ground, or pounded and boiled with meat of any sort, it makes a most nutritious meal. The potato, both Irish and sweet, forms an excellent substitute for bread. At Savannah we found that rice was also suitable, both for men and animals. For men, it should be cleaned of its husk in a hominy block, easily prepared out of a log, and sifted with a coarse corn bag. For horses it should be fed in the straw."

"During the Atlanta campaign we were supplied by our regular commissaries with all sorts of compounds, such as desiccated vegetables, concentrated milk, meat-biscuit, and sausages. We were also supplied liberally with lime-juice, sauerkraut, and pickles, as an antidote to scurvy, which at one time was spreading and imperiling the army. The railroad could not possibly bring us an adequate supply of potatoes and cabbage, but providentially the blackberries ripened and proved an admirable antidote. I have known the skirmish-line to fight a respectable battle for the possession of some old fields that were full of blackberries."

The young man who had posed the question about Hell on Earth, jumped to his feet and exclaimed, "But, General, I did not ask about blackberries. I asked you if you were sick of----"

Captain Rogers rose just as quickly to his feet and faced the graduates. "Let us all show General Sherman our deep appreciation for coming to the Academy today, and for spending this special time with all of us."

Rogers began loudly applauding his guest, and the sound spread across the room as the graduates joined in a firm round of applause for General Sherman.

As they were leaving the hall, Sherman bent slightly to whisper into Captain Rogers' ear, while holding him back by his left elbow.

"Please, Captain," he said. "Would you be so kind as to retrieve for me the name of that graduate from Virginia?"

"Certainly, General," Rogers replied. "I shall have it for you before the conclusion of lunch."

Post Script:

Ten years after the Civil War, William T. Sherman published his two volume Memoirs, in which he dispensed "military lessons" from the War. In 1883, Sherman relinquished his title as Commanding General of the Army and retired from his military career three months later. He moved to New York City, where he remained active in social life. The Republican party considered nominating Sherman for the President in the election of 1884, but Sherman insisted that he would not serve if elected. Sherman died in 1891 in New York City at the age of 71.

OPPENHEIMER'S PERSONAL BOMB

In early December of 1953, Major General Kenneth "Nick" Nichols, General manager of the U.S. Atomic Energy Commission, met for lunch with William Lisom Borden, the former executive director of Congress' Joint Committee on Atomic Energy. The JCAE, created in 1946, was the Congressional Committee with jurisdiction over all matters" related to civilian and military aspects of nuclear power. It had oversight of the Atomic Energy Commission.

Nichols had invited Borden to join him for a working lunch at the Occidental Grill on Pennsylvania Ave, in Washington, D.C., just around the corner from the White House. He told Borden he wanted discuss the status of J. Robert Oppenheimer, the Jewish-American scientist who had headed the Los Alamos Laboratory during World War II, and who played a key role in the top-secret Manhattan Project that produced the atomic bomb.

Oppenheimer, who was turning 50 years old, was one of the most famous scientists in America—yet doubts had been raised about his reputed involvement with the Communist Party. The Atomic Energy Commission was actively considering stripping Oppenheimer of his security clearance.

Major General Nichols was dressed in civilian clothes. He had a pleasant round face, most memorable for its pencil-thin mustache. Borden, like many other Capitol Hill staffers, wore a moderately expensive dark suit with a red tie and an American flag pin in his lapel.

Nichols had reserved his favorite secluded table in a corner of the restaurant, surrounded by framed celebrity photos of Llewelyn Adams, George Aiken, and George S. Patton. Over a white linen table cloth lunch of Maryland She Crab Bisque, Herb Crusted Tuna Loin and New Brunswick Salmon, Nichols explained the reason for summoning Borden.

"Bill, the AEC appreciates the work you've been doing on the Oppenheimer case," Nichols began, "I wanted to have the chance to update you on the hearings coming up this April."

"Thanks, Nick," Borden said. "I appreciate the invitation."

"Let me say right off the bat, Bill, that the letter you sent to the FBI in November regarding Bob Oppenheimer and the Soviets was extremely helpful. Hoover himself forwarded to it me and said his agency's surveillance was accurately reported in your letter. The Director said your recounting of the history of this affair was thorough and accurate."

"I'm glad to hear that," Borden replied. "As I said in my letter, my own considered opinion--based on exhaustive years of study—is that the available classified evidence shows, more probably than not, that J. Robert Oppenheimer was an agent of the Soviet Union. It's a little intimidating to bring such accusations against the scientist who ran the Los Alamos Lab and was widely credited for the success of the Manhattan Project and the atomic bomb---credits I don't think he fully deserves. My research showed me a very different side of Robert Oppenheimer, someone who poses a clear danger to our nation."

"Director Hoover felt strongly enough about your evidence that he asked the AEC to take direct action," Nichols added. "I wanted to tell you what we have done to date."

Drawing on the tablecloth with his finger, the Major General outlined his action plan: "First, a few days before Christmas, Commissioner Strauss, on behalf of the AEC, is going to notify Oppenheimer that his security file has become the subject of two recent re-evaluations. He will say it's because of new screening criteria, and because a former government official—we will not name you---has drawn attention to his record. Strauss will inform Oppenheimer that his clearance has been suspended, pending resolution of the charges, which will be outlined in a letter. Second, Strauss will ask him to resign, and give him a day or two to think it over. We feel certain he will not resign. The irony is that Oppenheimer's contract with the AEC expires at the end of June, 1954."

"He won't step down without a battle," Borden interrupted. "I know enough about him to predict that."

"Agreed. We expect Oppenheimer to invoke his right to a hearing," Nichols continued, "and we have already reserved time in early April to conduct the hearing---on a classified basis—at our AEC headquarters. If he chooses not to ask for a hearing, then the matter will be concluded and his security clearance will be over."

"He will fight you," Borden said. "His work is his life."

"My office has begun briefing our attorneys about questions for our direct examination. We will come at him with a full arsenal, I assure you. We can show that Oppenheimer's conduct reflected a serious disregard for the requirements of our security system; that he was susceptible to influence which could have serious implications for the security interests of the nation; and that his attitude toward the H-bomb program raised doubt about whether his future participation would be consistent with the best interests of security."

"Do you know if he has seen my letter?" Borden asked.

"I don't believe Hoover has shared it with anyone else outside of us."

"I don't want Oppenheimer to send his 'Red Army' friends after me..."

"I don't think you have anything to worry about, but if you have concerns," Nichols said, "I can ask for a protective detail from Director Hoover."

Both men turned their attention to their meals. Nichols ordered two Jefferson bourbons for the table. When the drinks arrived, Nichols made a toast "To the Personnel Security Hearings," and then picked up the conversation again:

"I'd like to show you a draft of the letter that Gordon Gray, as Chairman of the Personnel Security Board, is going to hand Oppenheimer and his counsel at the hearing."

"Who's his lawyer?" Borden asked.

"He's got Lloyd Garrison, Sam Silverman, and Allen Ecker."

"Mostly Jews, no doubt," Borden replied. "And who sits on the Personnel Security Board?"

"Gordon Gray will chair, plus Ward Evans and Tom Morgan," Nichols said. "We've got two solid votes before the hearings even get started. Evans is the only rogue member on the Board. But Oppenheimer is facing 24 separate charges. I expect most of them to stick."

"Who are the Board's lawyers?" Borden inquired.

"Counsel to the Board is Roger Robb and C.A. Rolander," Nichols added. "We've got a strong offensive team."

Major General Nichols unsnapped his leather briefcase on the chair to his right, pulled out a manila folder, removed a document creased in half from his folder, and handed the document--marked "SECRET/DRAFT"--to Borden.

"This is labeled DRAFT for a reason, Bill. Chairman Strauss wanted me to ask you to look it over for accuracy. I can't let the letter out of my possession--

but Lewis wanted you to review it. This is first document that will be presented to Oppenheimer at the hearing."

Borden took the letter from Nichols and began reading it:

"SECRET/DRAFT   SECRET/DRAFT

December 23, 1953

Dr. J. R. Oppenheimer,
The Institute for Advanced Study
Princeton, New Jersey,

Dear Dr. Oppenheimer:

Section 10 of the Atomic Energy Act of 1946 places upon the Atomic Energy Commission the responsibility for assuring that individuals are employed by the Commission only when such employment will not endanger the common defense and security. In addition, Executive Order 10450 of April 27, 1953, requires the suspension of employment of any individual where there exists information indicating that his employment may not be clearly consistent with the interests of the national security.

As a result of additional investigation as to your character, associations and loyalty, and review of your personnel security file in the light of the requirements of the Atomic Energy Act and the requirements of Executive Order 10450, there has developed considerable question whether your continued employment on Atomic Energy Commission work will endanger the common defense and security and whether such continued employment is clearly consistent with the interests of the national security.

The substance of the information which raises the question concerning your eligibility for employment on Atomic Energy Commission work is as follows:

It was reported that in 1940 you were listed as a sponsor of the Friends of the Chinese People, an organization which was characterized in 1944 by the House Committee on Un-American Activities as a Communist front organization.

It was further reported that in 1940 your name was included on a letterhead of the American Committee for Democratic and Intellectual Freedom as a member of its National Executive Committee, The American Committee for Democracy and Intellectual Freedom was characterized in 1942 by the House Committee on Un-American Activities as a Communist front which defended Communist teachers, and in 1943 it was characterized as subversive and un-American by a Special Subcommittee of the House Committee on Appropriations.

It was further reported that in 1938 you were a member of the Western Council of the Consumers Union. The Consumers Union was cited in 1944 by the House Committee on Un-American Activities as a Communist front headed by the Communist Arthur Kallet.

It was further reported that you stated in 1943 that you were not a Communist---but had probably belonged to every Communist front organization on the west coast and had signed many petitions in which Communists were interested.

It was reported that in 1943 and previously you were intimately associated with Dr. Jean Tatlock, a member of the Communist Party in San Francisco, and that Dr. Tatlock was partially responsible for your association with Communist front groups.

It was reported that your wife, Katherine Puening Oppenheimer, was formerly the wife of Joseph Dallet, a member of the Communist Party, who was killed in Spain in 1937 fighting for the Spanish Republican Army.

It was further reported that during the period of her association with Joseph Dallet your wife became a member of the Communist Party. The Communist Party has been designated by the Attorney General as a subversive organization which seeks to alter the form of Government of the United States by unconstitutional means, within the purview of Executive Order 9835 and Executive Order 10450.

It was reported that your brother Frank Friedman Oppenheimer became a member of the Communist Party in 1936 and has served as a Party organizer and as Educational Director of the Professional Section of the Communist Party in Los Angeles County.

It was further reported that your brother's wife, Jackie Oppenheimer, was a member of the Communist Party in 1938; and that in August, 1944, Jackie

Oppenheimer assisted in the organization of the East Bay branch of the California Labor School.

It was further reported that in 1945 Frank and Jackie Oppenheimer were invited to an informal reception at the Russian Consulate, that this invitation was extended by the American-Russian Institute of San Francisco and was for the purpose of introducing famous American scientists to Russian scientists who were delegates to the United Nations Conference on International Organization being held at San Francisco at that time, and that Frank Oppenheimer accepted this invitation.

It was further reported that Frank Oppenheimer agreed to give a six weeks course on "The Social Implications of Modern Scientific Development" at the California Labor School, beginning May 9, 1946. The American-Russian Institute of San Francisco and the California Labor School have been cited by the Attorney General as Communist organizations within the purview of Executive Order 9835 and Executive Order 10450.

It was reported that you have associated with members and officials of the Communist Party including Isaac Folkoff, Steve Nelson, Rudy Lambert, Kenneth May, Jack Manley, and Thomas Addis.

It was reported that you were a subscriber to the *Daily People's World*, a west coast Communist newspaper, in 1941 and 1942.

It was reported in 1950 that you stated to an agent of the Federal Bureau of Investigation that you had in the past made contributions to Communist front organizations, although at the time you did not know of Communist Party control or extent of infiltration of these groups. You further stated to an agent of the Federal Bureau of Investigation that some of these contributions were made through Isaac Folkoff, whom you knew to be a leading Communist Party functionary, because you bad been told that this was the most effective and direct way of helping these groups.

It was reported that you attended a housewarming party at the home of Kenneth and Ruth May on September 20, 1941, for which there was an admission charge for the benefit of *The People's World*, and that at this party you were in the company of Joseph W. Weinberg and Clarence Hiskey, who were alleged to be members of the Communist Party and to have engaged in espionage on behalf of the Soviet Union. It was further reported that you informed officials of the United States Department of Justice in

1952 that you had no recollection that you had attended such a party, but that since it would have been in character for you to have attended such a party, you would not deny that you were there.

It was reported that you attended a closed meeting of the professional section of the Communist Party of Alameda County, California, which was held in the latter part of July or early August 1941, at your residence, 10 Kenilworth Court, Berkeley, California, for the purpose of hearing an explanation of a change in Communist Party Policy.

It was reported that you denied that you attended such a meeting and that such a meeting was held in your home.

It was reported that you stated to an agent of the Federal Bureau of Investigation in 1950, that you attended a meeting in 1940 or 1941, which may have taken place at the home of Haakon Chevalier, which was addressed by William Schneiderman, whom you knew to be a leading functionary of the Communist Party. In testimony in 1950 before the California State Senate Committee on Un-American Activities, Haakon Chevalier was identified as a member of the Communist Party in the San Francisco area in the early 1940's.

It was reported that you have consistently denied that you have ever been a member of the Communist Party.

It was further reported, that during the period 1942-1945 various officials of the Communist Party, including Dr. Hannah Peters, organizer of the Professional Section of the Communist Party, Alameda County, California, Bernadette Doyle, secretary of the Alameda County Communist Party, Steve Nelson, David Adelson, Paul Pinsky, Jack Manley, and Katrina Sandow, are reported to have made statements indicating that you were then a member of the Communist Party; that you could not be active in the Party at that time; that your name should be removed from the Party mailing list and not mentioned in any way; that you had talked the atomic bomb question over with Party members during this period; and that several years prior to 1945 you had told Steve Nelson that the Army was working on an atomic bomb. You stated in August of 1943 that you knew several individuals then at Los Alamos who had been members of the Communist Party. You did not, however, identify such former members of the Communist Party to the appropriate authorities.

It was also reported that during the period 1942-1945 you were responsible for the employment on the atom bomb Project of individuals who were members of the Communist Party or closely associated with activities of the Communist Party. It was reported that you stated to representative of the Federal Bureau of Investigation on September 5, 1946, that you had attended a meeting in the East Bay and a meeting in San Francisco at which there were present persons definitely identified with the Communist Party. When asked the purpose of the East Bay meeting and the identity of those in attendance you declined to answer on the ground that this had no bearing on the matter of interest being discussed.

It was reported in 1946 that you were listed as Vice Chairman on the letterhead of the Independent Citizens Committee of the Arts, Sciences, and Professions, Inc., which has been cited as a Communist front by the House Committee on Un-American Activities.

It was further reported that upon your return to Berkeley following your separation from the Los Alamos Project, you were visited by Haakon Chevalier on several occasions: and that your wife was in contact with Haakon and Barbara Chevalier in 1946 and 1947.

It was reported that in 1945 you expressed the view that "there is a reasonable possibility that it (the hydrogen bomb) can be made," but that the feasibility of the hydrogen bomb did not appear, on theoretical grounds, as certain as the fission bomb appeared certain, on theoretical grounds, when the Los Alamos Laboratory was started.

It was further reported that in the Autumn of 1949, and subsequently, you strongly opposed the development of the hydrogen bomb: (1) on moral grounds, (2) by claiming that it was not feasible; (3) by claiming that there were insufficient facilities and scientific personnel to carry on the development., and (4) that it was not politically desirable. It was further reported that even after it was determined, as a matter of national policy, to proceed with development of a hydrogen bomb, you continued to oppose the project and declined to cooperate fully in the project.

It was further reported that you departed from your proper role as an advisor to the Commission by causing the distribution separately, and in private, to top personnel at Los Alamos of the majority and minority reports of the General Advisory Committee on development of the hydrogen bomb for the purpose of trying to turn such top personnel against the development of the hydrogen bomb. It was further reported that you were instrumental in persuading other outstanding scientists not to work on the hydrogen bomb project, and that the opposition to the hydrogen bomb, of which you are the most experienced, most powerful, and most effective member, has definitely slowed down its development.

In view of your access to highly sensitive classified information, and in view of these allegations which---until disproved---raise questions as to your veracity, conduct, and even your loyalty, the Commission has no other recourse, in discharge of its obligations to protect the common defense and security, but to suspend your clearance until the matter has been resolved.

Accordingly, your employment on Atomic Energy Commission work and your eligibility for access to Restricted Data are hereby suspended, effective immediately, pending final determination of this matter."

When he came to the end, Borden refolded the letter in half, and handed the letter back to Nichols. He took a sip of bourbon.

"I'm glad you included the piece about his mistress," Borden said. "Tatlock was having an affair with Oppenheimer when he was teaching physics at Berkeley in '36. She was a med student at Stanford at the time. Neither she nor Oppenheimer knew they were under surveillance by the FBI and Army agents, or that their phones were tapped. It was Tatlock who introduced Oppenheimer to Communist Party members. They kept seeing each other for five years---even after Oppenheimer married Kitty Harrison."

"Tatlock committed suicide about ten years ago." Nichols added.

Both men were silent. A mantle clock chiming in the distance was the only sound crossing the room. A cold winter light reflected off the glass covered portraits hung tightly-packed on every wall.

"As I told Hoover," Borden said, "this whole Oppenheimer matter is detestable to me. The central problem is not whether he was ever a Communist. The existing evidence makes abundantly clear that he was. The central problem is assessing the degree of likelihood that he became an actual espionage and policy instrument of the Soviets. My opinion was that--more probably than not--the worst was the truth. I felt a duty simply to state to the responsible head of the security agency the conclusions which I have painfully crystallized. I believe any fair-minded man thoroughly familiar with the evidence must also be driven to accept."

"What do you think is going to happen next?" Borden asked.

"I think J. Robert Oppenheimer is going to see this whole thing explode right in his face," Nichols said, grimly. "His career is over. This is going to be his own personal atom bomb."

The Major General waived over the waiter and ordered two Almond Bread Puddings, and two Cirrus Vodkas.

When the desserts and cocktails arrived, Nichols lifted his glass and proposed another toast, and Borden also raised his glass into the air.

"To the Atom Bomb," Nichols said, "and To Surveillance Well Done! As the Russians say: "За здоровье!"

Both men drained their vodkas, and gently lay their glasses back on the white linen.

Post Script:

The AEC Personnel Security Board hearing regarding J. Robert Oppenheimer was held behind closed doors for over four weeks. Oppenheimer testified for 27 hours. At the conclusion of the panel's deliberations, Oppenheimer was stripped of his Department of Energy Q Clearance, formally ending his long-standing service to the U.S. Government. The decision against him was on a two to one vote of the panel. Retired industrialist Thomas Morgan, and University of North Carolina president Gordon Gray voted to revoke Oppenheimer's security clearance. Ward Evans, chair of the Northwestern University Chemistry Department, voted to keep Oppenheimer's clearance. The panel concluded that Oppenheimer was neither disloyal to his country, nor improperly handled atomic secrets---but they recommended his security clearance be terminated.

Three years later, Oppenheimer was awarded the Legion of Honor by France, made a Member of the Royal Society in England, and in 1963, U.S. President John F. Kennedy awarded Oppenheimer the Enrico Fermi Award for his contribution to theoretical physics. Oppenheimer was the 7th scientist to receive this honor, which came with a gold medal and a $50,000 stipend. German-American rocket scientist Wernher von Braun testified before Congress that, "In England, Oppenheimer would have been knighted." Oppenheimer died in New Jersey in 1967 at the age of 62.

The complete transcripts of the Oppenheimer hearings were not released until 2012, 45 years after this death.

William Lisom Borden died in 1985 at the age of 65

BUILDERS OF THE BEAUTIFUL WORLD

"I would rather a thousand times be a free soul in jail, than to be a sycophant and coward in the streets."

Eugene V. Debs had been invited to speak at an anti-war rally in Canton, Ohio in 1918. He was 63 years old and had run for President of the United States as a candidate of the Socialist Party in 1900, 1904, 1908, and 1912. He knew that every speech he gave was being watched by the government. "I must be exceedingly careful, prudent, as to what I say," he told the crowd, "and even more careful and prudent as to how I say it. I may not be able to say all I think---but I am not going to say anything that I do not think."

Debs grew up in a prosperous family in Terre Haute, Indiana. His father, owned a textile mill and meat market. Debs dropping out of high school at age 14. He took a job cleaning railroad freight cars, and when he was 20 years old, became a member of the Brotherhood of Locomotive Firemen and over twenty years there he rose to be the union's Grand Secretary and Treasurer. He also immersed himself in local civic life, elected twice as the City Clerk of Terre Haute. At age 29 Debs was elected on the Democratic ticket as a member of the Indiana General Assembly. He went on to help found the American Railway Union, one of the first industrial unions in America.

It was a warm afternoon in Canton. Debs was on the podium in his shirtsleeves, cuffs rolled up.

"They may put some of us in jail," Debs warned, "but they cannot put the Socialist movement in jail. Those prison bars separate their bodies from ours, but their souls are here this afternoon. They are simply paying the penalty that all men have paid in all the ages of history for standing erect, and for seeking to pave the way to better conditions for mankind. If it had not been for the men and women who, in the past, have had the moral courage to go to jail, we would still be in the jungles."

Debs knew all about going to jail. In 1894, he and other leaders of the American Railway Union had been jailed as a consequence of the Pullman railway strike. The following year he was jailed in Woodstock, Illinois, where he served six months for contempt of court in connection with the Pullman strike. For his Canton, Ohio speech, Debs would be given a ten-year jail sentence.

"In the Republican and Democratic parties, you of the common herd are not expected to think," Debs told his Canton audience. "That is what the 'intellectual' leaders are for. They do the thinking and you do the voting. They ride in carriages at the front where the band plays and you tramp in the mud, bringing up the rear with great enthusiasm. When we have ventured to say to the capitalists that the time would come when the working class would rule, they have bluntly answered 'Never! It requires brains to rule.' The workers of course have none. And they certainly try hard to prove it by proudly supporting the political parties of their masters under whose administration they are kept in poverty and servitude."

"War comes, in spite of the people. When Wall Street says war, the press says war and the pulpit promptly follows with its Amen. In every age the pulpit has been on the side of the rulers and not on the side of the People. In good time we are going to sweep into power in this nation and throughout the world. We are going to destroy all enslaving and degrading capitalist institutions and re-create them as free and humanizing institutions."

"The world is daily changing before our eyes. The sun of capitalism is setting; the sun of socialism is rising. It is our duty to build the new nation and the free republic. We need industrial and social builders. We Socialists are the builders of the beautiful world that is to be. In due time the hour will strike and this great cause triumphant—the greatest in history—will proclaim the emancipation of the working class and the brotherhood of all mankind."

Debs was convicted in federal court in Cleveland under the war-time espionage law. He represented himself in court. In April of 1919 he began serving his sentence in Moundsville, West Virginia state prison. He was transferred two months later to the federal penitentiary in Atlanta, Georgia.

The warden of the Moundsville prison, Joseph Terrell, wrote a letter to the warden in Atlanta about Eugene Debs. "I never met in my life a kinder man." Terrell admitted. "He is forever thinking of others, trying to serve them, and never thinking of himself."

The federal jail in Atlanta was a medium-security facility, a more hardened institution. The Atlanta site was the largest Federal prison, with a capacity of 3,000 inmates. Inmate case files were kept on all men confined in the penitentiary: their medical records, their letters, and their visitors.

While Debs was in an Atlanta prison cell, he was nominated—for the fifth time—to run for President of the United States at the top of the Socialist Party ticket. Debs planned to run his campaign by issuing a weekly statement, which he wrote from his cell, and each week he mailed them to his home in Terre Haute, where they were typed up and sent to the national office of the Socialist Party in Chicago, and from there distributed to the press and to Party newspapers.

In April of 1920, Debs was visited in the penitentiary by two old friends: Victor Berger, who was a founding member of the Social Democratic Party, and who a decade earlier had become the first Socialist elected to the House of Representatives in Congress, representing a district in Milwaukee, Wisconsin, and George Washington Howard who was the Vice President of the American Railway Union under Debs, and who was the first American prisoner to be confined in Joliet prison as a result of the Pullman strike.

Berger and Howard proposed that they do a "jailhouse interview" with Debs to be widely circulated to the newspapers and magazines in the run-up to the 1920 election. They brought along a stenographer to keep a verbatim record of what Debs said in response to their questions.

Victor Berger began the interview by asking Debs: "There was an editorial recently which said that 'Debs started for the White House, but he only got as far as the federal prison.' What is your reaction to that?"

"I am not the least perturbed by that comment," Debs said. "I knew in advance that my course led, not to the presidential mansion, but through the prison gates. I had already been the candidate of the socialist party in four previous campaigns for President. It may or may not be an enviable distinction to be nominated for the high office of President of the United States while in the garb of a felon and serving a term as such in one of its penitentiaries."

"I was amused by one newspaper wag who said at the beginning of the campaign that my opponent, Mr. Cox, would make his speeches from the tail end of a train. Mr. Harding would appeal for votes from his front porch, while I would make my bid for the support of the electorate from a front cell. Having had almost a million votes cast for me in an earlier campaign-- and as many more that were not counted---and feeling that I had been more than sufficiently honored, I concluded not to be a presidential candidate again, and in the national political contest of 1916 I did not permit the use of my name in the nominations."

"When the time came for making the nominations for President in 1920, I was serving my sentence here in Atlanta prison. In response to urgent solicitations from the membership, at first, I positively declined to be considered a candidate. Later, however, when I was assured that the nomination would be made irrespective of my views in the matter--and that it would be unanimous--I yielded to the wishes of the delegates. The nomination followed and, as predicted, was made by acclamation in the convention held in New York City."

"Why were you reluctant to join the race for President this year," Howard asked.

"I had my own personal reasons for not wishing to be the standard bearer, reasons which dated back to the time when I was a member of the Indiana legislature. I made a resolution to myself that I would never again be a candidate for a public office, preferring to devote my energies to tasks immediately identified with the industrial side of the labor movement."

"The party to which I gave allegiance chose otherwise, thus setting aside my personal wishes. Men had been nominated for President who were born in log cabins to testify to their lowly origin, but never before had such a nomination been conferred upon an imprisoned convict. It was indeed an unprecedented distinction which had been bestowed upon me. I had a visit to the prison by the Socialist Committee on Notification. The federal government granted the necessary permission for such a committee to call upon me. The ceremony occurred in the warden's office."

"What was that ceremony like? Were the newspapers there?" Howard asked.

"Yes, representatives of the press were in the prison at the time and gave good accounts to their readers of the very unusual proceedings at the prison. The film photographers were also in eager evidence to pictorialize the event, and a few days later the scenes were reproduced on screens in thousands of motion picture theaters throughout the country. The warden permitted me to be escorted by the committee outside the prison gates where informal conversations were held, more pictures taken, and where a group of Atlanta children presented me with a bouquet of red roses."

"What were the reactions of your fellow inmates?" Berger wondered. "The whole scene must have seemed most strange to them."

"Never in all of my experience as a presidential candidate had I been so deeply touched and so profoundly impressed by the congratulations of friends as I was by those I received that day and in the days that followed from the inmates of the Atlanta federal prison. The hands--black and white--were extended to me from the cells and from all directions, while faces beamed with a warmth and sincerity that found expression from eager lips."

"The little speeches made by some of these poor broken brothers of mine to whom no nomination had ever come--save that issued by the judge who pronounced their doom--voiced genuine pride and joy in the honor which had come to me, evincing a beautiful and generous human spirit that, in spite of its hardening and degrading conditions, the prison could not extinguish. I felt more highly honored by these manifestations of my fellow convicts, on account of their obvious unselfishness, their spontaneous and generous enthusiasm, than any congratulatory occasion I had ever before experienced."

"I imagine that if the vote had been held here in this penitentiary—that you would be the overwhelming victor," Berger said.

Debs laughed at the thought.

"One of the popular comments heard in the course of the prison campaign was that I was certain to sweep every precinct in the penitentiary--and that neither Mr. Harding nor Mr. Cox--my political adversaries--would receive a single prison electoral vote."

"If you could talk directly to the American voters this morning, what would you tell them?" Howard asked.

"I am the candidate of the Socialist party for president of the United States. I hope you know me well enough to know that I am not a candidate because I want office. Had I wanted office I would not be a socialist. I would have remained in the Democratic Party and gloried in its rottenness."

"The workers have a majority of votes. They outnumber their masters, and bosses overwhelmingly at the polls. There they are masters, if they only will. The Republican and Democratic Parties are Wall Street's political twins; they do the dirty work in the dirty system of which they are the dirty products. They are as near alike as corruption is to corruption and rottenness to rottenness, and there is between them an equal exchange of both in every campaign. They both stand for capitalism and exploitation, for the supremacy of the capitalist class and the slavery of the working class."

"I am not asking you workers to vote for me. I am asking you to think for yourselves and refuse any longer to be deceived and delivered, like live stock by crooked politicians and lying newspapers. Ever since my boyhood I have been in your struggle. I am in it now. I shall be in it until the breath leaves my body. There is no other place for me."

"I can talk plainly to you, men and women of labor. We have been in the trenches together. I have seen your hunger and thirst. I have seen you in rags, you and your wife and child. I have seen you battling for bread, and I have been with you when the blood trickled down your furrowed cheek. I have seen your matted, bloody head and the bullet wounds in your body as you fought the gunmen of your masters. I have seen you at bay with a dangerous glint in your eyes. I have seen you turned out of a job into the street for being a man. I have seen you blacklisted and your children starved because you refused to be a dog."

"I have seen you a tramp, an outcast, sharing your crust with your pal in rags. I have seen you in jail, beaten by a brute into insensibility in the name of the law. I have seen you in the penitentiary, a branded convict, shorn of every right to be a man, and everywhere my heart has been with you. Everywhere I felt the blows that fell upon your head and the bullets that pierced your body. Everywhere you were my brother and I loved you, and never in my life have I loved you as I love you now, behind these walls, where there are so many of our class who fell in the tragic battle for bread, to keep me company."

Berger and Howard put down their pencils. The stenographer lifted her fingers from her machine. "Wonderful words," Berger said in admiration. "We will get this into the hands of the press as soon as we can."

"Do you want more?" Debs asked. "There is more I want to say."

"Yes, of course," Howard said. Berger nodded.

"When great changes occur in history, when great principles are involved, as a rule the majority are wrong. But there is nothing in our government it cannot remove or amend. It can make and unmake Presidents and Congresses and Courts. It can abolish unjust laws and consign to eternal odium and oblivion unjust judges, strip from them their robes and gowns and send them forth unclean as lepers to bear the burden of merited obloquy as Cain with the mark of a murderer."

"It can sweep our trusts, syndicates, corporations, monopolies and every other abnormal development of the money power designed to abridge the liberties of workingmen and enslave them by the degradation incident to poverty and enforced idleness as cyclones scatter the leaves of our forest. The ballot can do all this and more. It can give our civilization its crowning glory--the co-operative commonwealth. I am opposing a social order in which it is possible for one man who does absolutely nothing that is useful to amass a fortune of hundreds of millions of dollars, while millions of men and women who work all the days of their lives secure barely enough for a wretched existence. I have no country to fight for. My country is the earth. I am a citizen of the world. Years ago, I recognized my kinship with all living beings and I made up my mind that I was not one bit better than the meanest on earth. While there is a lower class, I am in it. While there is a criminal element, I am of it. And while there is a soul in prison, I am not free."

"My eyes have been opened and I know better now. We are all one, and there is nothing we cannot do. We are the people and we have all power, IF WE ARE UNITED. We are slaves only as long as we are divided."

At the end of their meeting, Berger put on his coat jacket, and came over to Debs.

"No matter what happens on election night," Berger said, embracing Debs, "you will be a winner. You know they voted last January to deny me my seat in Congress and left my seat vacant rather than see me fill it. As long as capitalism lasts, the speculators are absolutely necessary to protect the system from stagnation. This is another evil that is inherent in this system. It cannot be avoided any more than malaria in a swampy country. And the speculators are the mosquitos. We should have to drain the swamp---change the capitalist system---if we want to get rid of those mosquitos. Teddy Roosevelt, by starting a little fire here and there to drive them out, is simply disturbing them. He is causing them to swarm, which makes it so much more intolerable for us poor, innocent inhabitants of this big capitalist swamp. I will be with you in spirit, Gene, on election evening..."

Eight months later, on election night, after the supper hour, Debs was visited by the Deputy Warden, Charles Girardeau, a man who had a reputation for unbridled brutality and sadism. Girardeau took him into the office of Warden Fred B. Zerbst to hear the returns that were being received by telephone and in the form of special messages. Warden Zerbst and his wife were present, along with members of the press. As the bulletins came in, Debs spread them out across the table.

Early in the evening, Debs conceded the election of Warren G. Harding as President. He told his fellow inmates that his defeat excited no surprise among those in the prison office. "The only surprise," Debs said, "was that felt in some of the prison cells."

"An interesting question arose," Debs wrote later to his family, "while we sat there in the warden's office, as to a pardon from myself in the event of my election. We all found some mirth in debating it. I am sure the question did not disturb my slumber in the nights preceding this particular one."

Debs remained in Warden Zerbst's office until Harding's election was officially confirmed. "I was not elected President," he joked with Zerbst, "but in the next few hours I will be in dreamland sailing the seven seas in quest of new worlds to conquer."

"Before you head off to dreamland," Warden Zerbst said, "we should discuss, Mr. Debs, the subject of your pardon. You are now 65 years old, and I believe the subject of pardons will come across President Wilson's desk."

Debs looked surprised. When he was in Woodstock prison years ago, Debs had said he would not seek a pardon for himself until all were pardoned. But he was facing eight more years in Atlanta. If nothing changed, he might never again see his wife and family outside of the granite walls of this penitentiary.

"What have you heard?" Debs asked Zerbst. It suddenly occurred to Debs that his future depended on this man in front of him whom he hardly knew, other than the details of his rise in the penal system.

Frederick G. Zerbst was considered a highly formal, but likeable man. He became warden at the Atlanta penitentiary at the age of 49. Debs grasped that this man Zerbst would be asked by the White House for a recommendation regarding his pardon. What had he told the White House?

"President Wilson will not grant you a pardon," Zerbst flatly told him. "He is an embittered man. He will not forgive those who opposed him. Your friends who are arguing for your release are not helping your cause."

"How so?" Debs asked.

"They say your pardon is justified, because your imprisonment creates bitterness amongst millions of sympathizers," Zerbst replied. "They charge that such punishment for making a speech is excessive, particularly when there are businesses that are doing the masses of the people so much real harm through their arbitrary and outrageously extortionate profit extractions—and they seem to be entirely immune from either restraint or punishment."

"They say your prosecution was actuated by your concern for the public welfare, while no appreciable effort has been made---or is being made—-by government authorities to restrain the plundering of profiteers. They say your advanced years and physical infirmities have made imprisonment a fatal sentence to you. They say the war is over, and the need for such punishments occasioned by the war no longer exists."

"And finally, they say that Mr. Debs did not do anything, but simply said something. He did not influence his hearers by what he said, as practically all of them already agreed with the views expressed."

At this last comment, Debs broke out in a surprised laugh. "Ha! That statement hits the mark! I often thought I was preaching to the converted. But you tell me my supporters have said all this, and more?"

"Yes, your case has caused much ink to be spilled, Mr. Debs," Zerbst said. "I would counsel you to throw yourself at Wilson's feet, and apologize for your actions, and your inflammatory words."

"That," Debs assured him, "I cannot do, and I never shall do."

"Then you shall die within these walls, and never again enjoy the comforts of your family and your home in Terre Haute," Zerbst said with sadness. "Or, in the alternative, you can wait for affable Warren G. Harding to occupy the White House, and have your friends ply their arguments with him. I am told he wants to meet the famous Eugene Debs. This may be your best option at this point..."

Zerbst shook Debs' hand and wished him a good night.

Deputy Warden Girardeau, who had been waiting outside the Warden's office, escorted Debs back to his cell in the second tier of the main wing.

As a guard was unlocking Debs' cell, Deputy Warden Girardeau gave Debs a slight inward push from the middle of his back. "Have a pleasant night's sleep, Mr. President," the Deputy Warden mocked. "Perhaps your 6th try for high office will bring you more luck. How many times can you continue to present yourself to the American people after such total rejection as you have witnessed this evening? I fear that in 1924 I will still be looking through these bars at your wretched socialist face."

And with that, he slammed the iron door shut, and left Eugene V. Debs to drift off to dreamland and the seven seas.

Post Script:

In 1919, President Woodrow Wilson wrote of Debs: "This man was a traitor to his country and he will never be pardoned during my administration."

Just before Christmas of 1921, incoming President Warren Harding decided not to issue a pardon, but instead to commute Debs' sentence to time served. The White House issued a statement that said Debs "is an old man, not strong physically. He is a man of much personal charm and impressive personality..."

Immediately following his release, Debs traveled to the White House at the invitation of President Harding, who said "I've heard so damned much about you, Mr. Debs, that I am now glad to meet you personally."

Upon his return home to Terre Haute, Indiana, Debs was met by a crowd of 50,000 supporters. Three years later he was nominated for the Nobel Peace Prize.

Debs died in an Illinois hospital in 1926, at the age of 70.

AGENT ELVIS

A 'Jon Burrows' checked into the Washington Hotel in the nation's capital on a cold day in December of 1970. He had arrived at National Airport on an overnight flight from L.A. He had in his pocket a letter he had written on American Airlines stationery addressed to President Richard Nixon, which he marked "Private and Confidential":

"Dear Mr. President,

First, I would like to introduce myself. I am Elvis Presley and admire you and have great respect for your office. I talked to Vice President Agnew in Palm Springs three weeks ago and expressed my concern for our country. The Drug Culture, The Hippie Elements, The SDS, Black Panthers, etc. Do not consider me as their enemy or as they call it The Establishment. I call it America and I love it. Sir I can and will be of any Service that I can to help the Country out. I have no concerns or motives other than helping the country out. So, I wish not to be given a title or an appointed position. I can and will do more good if I were made a Federal Agent at Large, and I will help best by doing it my way through my communications with people of all ages. First and foremost, I am an entertainer, but all I need is the Federal credentials...I have two men who work with me by the name of Gerry Schilling and Sonny West. I am registered [at the Washington Hotel] under the name of Jon Burrows. I will be here for as long as it takes to get the credentials of a Federal agent. I have done an in-depth study of Drug Abuse and Communist Brainwashing Techniques and I am right in the middle of the whole thing, where I can and will do the most good. I am glad to help just so long as it is kept very Private. You can have your staff or whomever call me anytime today tonight or tomorrow. I was nominated the coming year as one of America's Ten Most Outstanding young men. That will be in January 18 in my Home Town of Memphis Tenn. I am sending you the short autobiography about myself so you can better understand this approach. I would love to meet you just to say hello if you're not too Busy.

Respectfully,

Elvis Presley

P.S. I believe that you Sir were one of the Top Ten Outstanding Men of America also. I have a personal gift for you also which I would like to present to you and you can accept it or I will keep it for you until you can take it."

'Burrows,' and his aide, Jerry Schilling, took a limo from the airport, past the Lincoln Memorial, down Pennsylvania Avenue to the White House. Burrows had not told Shilling about the purpose of the visit. He handed Schilling the note he had written on the plane and asked him to hand it to the guard.

The two men then rode back to the Washington Hotel, dropped off their luggage in their room, got back into the limo, and went to the Bureau of Narcotics and Dangerous Drugs, which had just been created by Congress two years earlier.

Burrows asked for a meeting with a Deputy Director of the agency. He told the officer at the Security Desk that his name was Elvis Presley and showed him his Memphis driver's license. A short impromptu meeting was arranged with a Deputy Director, who told Presley he was a great fan of his, but politely added that he did not have the authority to just give him a bureau badge.

Presley gently argued with the Deputy, showed him a few of the other police badges he had brought with him from Memphis, and told him, "I could do a lot for this country if I had a drug bureau badge." But the Deputy made it clear getting clearance for a badge was above his pay grade—even for the King of Rock 'N Roll.

Heading back to the hotel, Schilling asked Elvis directly: "What's the deal with this badge thing?"

"If I had a narcotic's agent badge," Elvis explained patiently, "I could enter any country I wanted, on any continent I wanted, wearing guns, and carrying any kind of drug you can name. It's the best passport a man could carry."

Schilling knew that Elvis had a large collection of police badges back in Memphis and had brought some of them to Washington. He also figured that people collect a lot of strange things, and what did it really matter to him. He dropped the subject as they arrived back at the hotel.

When Nixon aide Egil Krogh heard that someone claiming to be Elvis Presley had pulled up in a limousine at the west gate of the White House, leaving a handwritten message for the President, he reported the incident up the chain to Bob Haldeman, Chief of Staff. Krogh convinced Haldeman without too much effort that a Nixon-Presley meeting could have a great PR value if handled correctly. Haldeman instructed Krogh to phone the Washington Hotel and work out a meeting time with Schilling.

Elvis was thrilled. He asked Schilling, "Do you think I could give Nixon the Colt .45 pistol as a small gift—the one I had mounted on the wall in L.A.?" "Why not," answered Schilling. "It if means something to you, it should mean something to the President."

Elvis put on a purple velvet suit over his high collar white shirt, wore a gold chain around his neck and a longer, silver chain over his shirt, along with his over-sized gold belt buckle that he liked to call his "heavy-weight champ" buckle.

By midday, Elvis, Schilling, and bodyguard Sonny West—who had been summoned up from Memphis--were at the White House. The first thing the Secret Service did was take the Colt .45 away from Elvis for safe-keeping. They let him hold onto his small collection of police badges. Then Krogh took Elvis in to see the President. Schilling and West were told to remain behind in the hallway.

West turned to Schilling with a puzzled look. "Do you know what the heck we're here for? I asked Vernon and he had no clue."

"All I know." Schilling said in a low whisper, "is that I get this call to pick him up at the L.A. airport at 3 a.m. In the car he tells me that he and Priscilla and Vern had some words in Memphis. Apparently, they were both getting on him about all the money he spent on Christmas gifts. He bought like 10 Mercedes-Benzes, and 32 handguns. Vern was really lettin' him have it. Elvis got pissed and hopped on a plane. He tells me to meet him at the airport—but he doesn't say why."

"And what's all this shit about narcotics badges?" West asked.

"It's a power thing," Schilling said. "He wants to be able to carry drugs anywhere—and this badge tells the cops to let him alone."

"This is some crazy shit," West said, widening his eyes.

"I know. I feel like I'm dealing with a little child sometimes. Like a kid who wants to buy up badges at the Dime store to play Sheriff."

The two of them stood there in the White House hallway, looking at the oil paintings on the wall, the long curtains, and ornate gold chandeliers. They waited for what seemed like half an hour.

Elvis finally emerged with Krogh following behind.

Elvis was beaming, and had a kind of glassy, awe-struck appearance on his face. But he was broadly smiling.

"I showed him my police badges," Elvis said. "I told him the Beatles were spreading a lot of anti-American feelings. Especially John Lennon. The President said he knew that too. He told me that those hippies who are leading anti-American protests in the street are all drug abusers. That's when I told him, 'I'm on your side, Mr. President. I know this drug culture. It's a Communist brainwashing conspiracy. The Beatles are just talented drug pushers. Lennon is the worst of them.' I told him this British music has been a disaster for Memphis and the American music industry. I told the President we should have special agents tracking the whole lot of them, until we put them on a plane back to London. Then I asked him for a badge from the Bureau of Dangerous Drugs."

"And what did he say?" Schilling asked.

"He looked over at Krogh and said: 'Can we get him a badge?' And Krogh said 'Yes, we can. Mr. President.' And Nixon said, 'Let's do it then!'"

"Holy Mother," said West. "So, now you're Elvis the Agent!"

"Just as simple as that!" Elvis continued. "Then I put my arm around him and gave him a hug. I was afraid he might break."

The door to the Oval Office swung open, and Krogh came out. He waved to Schilling and West to step into the office, telling them the President had something for them.

"Mr. Presley told me you were here," Nixon said, coming from behind his desk. "I wanted to give you both a little token of this visit."

The President gave Schilling a playful jab to the shoulder, and then handed both men a pair of White House cufflinks in a plastic box.

"Mr. President, they have wives, too," Elvis said. Nixon turned to his staff and gave them a little thumbs-up sign. An aide went over to a shelf and came back with two little boxes.

"Give this to your wives," Nixon nodded, "and when you get back to Memphis, take good care of the King for me, won't you?"

The three visitors were ushered back into the hallway. West was the first to open his box. "What's this?" he asked Schilling.

"I think it's a brooch."

"A what?"

"It's a White House brooch for the ladies," said Krogh, leaning into the circle. "Designed by Pat Nixon."

Krogh then led the men down to the White House mess for a roast beef lunch. A staff person joined the party about twenty minutes later with a blue box that he handed Presley.

"Here's your 'narc badge'," Krogh said, handing it to Presley. "Directly by Presidential order."

"Please thank the President when you see him," Elvis said. "Tell him I will carry this proudly."

Presley grabbed Krogh's arm and pulled him close so he could whisper something meant only for him to hear. "Please," Presley said, "do me the favor of keeping this meeting secret. I don't want people to know I was here."

Outside the White House gate, Presley opened up his blue box and held up to the sun his new "narcotics badge," which flashed gold as he turned it.

"Eat your heart out, John Lennon," Elvis laughed. "Eat your fucking heart out."

Post Script:

In 1973 Elvis Presley overdosed on barbiturates twice, and was hospitalized a third time for a drug-related incident. In August of 1977, Presley was found unconscious on the bathroom floor of his home in Memphis. Lab reports suggested that the use of multiple medications was the primary cause of death. Presley had fourteen drugs in his system. He died at the age of 42. His funeral was held at Graceland.

When told about the discussion between Presley and Nixon, Beatles icon Paul McCartney said he "felt a bit betrayed. ...The great joke was that we were taking drugs and look what happened to him."

In 1976, Presley's father, Vernon Presley, fired Sonny West. The following year, West released a memoir entitled Elvis: What Happened? *which urged Presley to change his drug dependent lifestyle. The book sold over three million copies. Presley reportedly tried to pay the publisher to stop the publication of the book. Presley died two weeks after West's book was released. In 2007, Sonny West released a second book called* Elvis: Still Takin' Care of Business, *which focused on his relationship with Presley.*

After Presley's death, Jerry Schilling went on to manage the Beach Boys for more than a decade. He also managed Jerry Lee Lewis and Lisa Marie Presley, the performer's daughter. Presley bought Schilling a home. Schilling wrote a book called Me And A Guy Named Elvis.

CORMORANTS AND BLOODSUCKERS

"My head has been threatened," Andrew Johnson told the crowd gathered in downtown Cleveland.

It was the afternoon of September 3, 1866, the 8th stop on President Johnson's "Swing Around the Circle" 18-day speaking tour, which took his entourage on a giant loop from the White House north to Maryland, Pennsylvania and New York, west to Ohio and Michigan, south to Indiana and Kentucky, and then circling back east through Ohio and Pennsylvania, and returning to Washington, D.C.

Johnson undertook the campaign tour despite the cautions of his staff, who preferred the Chief Executive stay home in the White House. The President was facing rising disaffection in the Northern states due to his steadfast opposition to Republican plans for Reconstruction of the south after the War. Johnson, who had been raised in the South, favored policies which left the social system of the Confederacy largely untouched, keeping the same people in the same positions of power as before the War, and failing to advance the negro's status.

Andrew Johnson grew up in Raleigh, North Carolina. His family had little money. Instead of going to school, Johnson found work as a tailor's apprentice. He moved to Tennessee, got involved in small town politics, and was elected alderman and then Mayor of Greeneville. At the age of 27, he was elected to the Tennessee House of Representatives, and by age 35 had won the right to serve his Tennessee District in the U.S. House of Representatives, where he remained for ten years. He returned to his home state to run a successful campaign for Governor, and then the state legislature elected him to the U.S. Senate at the age of 49.

When Tennessee voted to secede from the Union, Johnson refused to support the Confederate States movement, and remained in the U.S. Senate. In 1864, Republican President Abraham Lincoln was looking to heal the nation's Civil War wounds. He liked the symbolism of reaching across the aisle to pick Andrew Johnson---a Southern Democrat and Union loyalist---for his Vice President in his Second Term.

Six weeks after the inauguration, Lincoln's assassination put Johnson in the White House.

But Johnson's hands-off approach to Reconstruction of the South disaffected him from many Lincoln Republicans. Johnson blundered politically when he came out in opposition to the 14th Amendment to the Constitution, which gave former slaves citizenship. He shunned legislation to continue the Freedman's Bureau, established in 1865 by Congress to help millions of former black slaves and poor whites in the South. Members of the House had begun talking about impeaching President Johnson.

Johnson saw the Circle tour as a way to win back the support of at least moderate Northern Republicans. Johnson hoped in the election of 1868 to run for President by rebuilding Lincoln's National Unity style coalition of Democrat and Republican.

Johnson had already spoken in Baltimore, Philadelphia, New York City, West Point, Albany, Niagara Falls and Buffalo. So far, the President seemed pleased with the public reception he received at each stop. But Midwest Cleveland had a different feel.

Johnson's aides predicted rising antagonism as the President moved to blunt the Republican's "Radical Reconstruction" program. Johnson stood on a balcony overlooking a rowdy crowd in Cleveland, working from only a speech outline. Johnson had been warned that the crowd was salted with hecklers who would try to goad him. His staff urged him to deliver a prepared address that went light on Reconstruction---but Johnson had confidence in his ability to give a stump speech.

"It has been said that my blood is to be shed," Johnson said, putting his right hand over his heart. "Let me say to those who are still willing to sacrifice my life: if you want a victim and my country requires it, erect your altar, and the individual who addresses you tonight---while here a visitor--- erect your altar if you still thirst for blood, and if you want it, take out the individual who now addresses you and lay him upon your altar, and the blood that now courses his veins and warms his existence shall be poured out as a last libation to Freedom."

There was a mixture of jeers and cheers from the crowd. It took a full minute for the commotion in the crowd to simmer down.

"I love my country," Johnson insisted, "and I defy any man to put his finger upon anything to the contrary. Then what is my offence?"

"You ain't no Radical Republican," one person shouted back. "Support the Freedmen's Bureau!" yelled another.

"Let's talk about that Freedmen's Bureau bill," Johnson challenged. "Before the Rebellion, there were four million colored persons held as slaves by about 340,000 people living in the South. That is, 340,000 slave owners paid expenses, bought land, and worked the negroes---and at the expiration of the year when cotton, tobacco, and rice were gathered and sold, after paying all expenses---these slave owners put the money in their pockets. In many instances there was no profit, and many came out in debt. Well, that is the way things stood before the Rebellion."

Johnson paused, and looked to see if he could tell where the growing clamor and confusion in the crowd was coming from. He thought about what his exit options were from the balcony, and where his key staff were placed.

"The Rebellion commenced," Johnson continued his story, "and the slaves were turned loose. Then we come to the Freedmen's Bureau bill. And what did the bill propose? It proposed to appoint agents and sub-agents in all the cities, counties, school districts, and parishes, with power to make contracts for all the slaves, power to control, and power to hire them out--dispose of them--and in addition to that, the whole military power of the government applied to carry it into execution."

The catcalls grew louder, and from several directions. Johnson wondered: Was he losing the crowd? Had he already lost them?

"Now to the Freedmen's Bureau: What was it? It was born in the Lincoln Administration, but now Congress seeks to expand it. Four million slaves were emancipated and given an equal chance and fair start to make their own support---to work and produce. And having worked and produced, to have their own property and apply it to their own support. But the Freedmen's Bureau comes and says: 'We must take charge of these 4 million slaves.' The Bureau comes along and proposes--at an expense of a fraction less than $12 million a year--to take charge of these slaves. You taxpayers had already expended $3 million to set them free and give them a fair opportunity to take care of themselves, then these gentlemen---who are such great friends of the people---tell us they must be taxed $12 million to sustain the Freedmen's Bureau."

"Congress now wants to provide many additional provisions for former slaves, including the distribution of land, schools for their children, and military courts to ensure these rights. Any of the civil rights or immunities belonging to white persons, including the right to inherit, purchase, lease, sell real and personal property, and to have full and equal benefit of all laws and proceedings affecting white people, including the constitutional right of bearing arms."

At this point, the yelling around him grew so loud he feared that most people assembled would fail to hear his words.

"Give Negroes the same rights you have!" one man shouted.

Johnson struggled vainly to regain the attention of his audience: "I would rather speak to 500 men who would give me their attention, than to 100,000 that would not."

Johnson's aides were nervously moving closer to the balcony.

"The Civil Rights bill was more enormous than the Freedmen's Bureau. I exercised the veto power, my critics say. Let me say to you of the threats from your Radical Republicans, who say the whole fabric of Southern society must be changed. I care not for such radicals. They once talked about forming a 'league with hell and a covenant with the devil.' I tell you, my countrymen, here tonight, though the power of hell and death, there is no power that can control me---save _you_ the people--and the God that spoke me into existence."

Johnson could see some pushing and shoving off to his right in the crowd. It looked like a wind that was swaying people back and forth, like a field of wheat.

"Because I stand now," Johnson said, raising his voice, with an outstretched arm, pointed to the heavens, "as I did when the Rebellion commenced, I have been denounced as a traitor. My countrymen here tonight: who has suffered more than I? Who has run greater risk? Who has borne more than I? But Congress---factious, domineering, tyrannical Congress---has undertaken to poison the minds of the American people and create a feeling against me in consequence of the manner in which I have distributed the public patronage."

One group of what his staff later called "goons" began pushing their way towards the balcony.

"While this gang--this common gang of cormorants and bloodsuckers--have been fattening upon the country for the past four of five years---men never going into the field, who growl at being removed from their fat offices---they are great patriots! Look at them all over your district! Everybody is a traitor that is against them. The time has come when those who stayed at home and enjoyed fat offices---I think it would be more than right for them to give way and let others participate in the benefits of office! I stood by the men who were in the field---and I stand by them now."

"It's time for *you* to stand down," one voice cried out. "You're the traitor here," another mocked.

The President picked up an American flag that had been folded on the chair beside him—a standard prop at such rallies--and began again:

"If I am insulted while civilities are going on, I will resent it in a proper manner, and in parting here tonight I have no anger nor revengeful feelings to gratify. All I want now---peace has come and the War is over---is for all patriotic men to rally round the standard of their country, and swear by their altars and their God, that all shall sink together but what this Union shall be supported."

Johnson unfolded his flag and held it out to the crowd as if an offering:

"In parting with you tonight, I hang over you this flag---not of 25 but of 36 stars. I hand over to you the Constitution of my country, though imprisoned, though breaches have been made upon it, with confidence hoping that you will repair the breaches. I hand it over to you, in whom I have always trusted and relied, and, so far, I have never deserted---and I feel confident, while speaking here tonight, for heart responds to heart of man, that you agree to the same great doctrine."

As Johnson's voice trailed off, someone in the crowd yelled "Hang Jeff Davis!" Johnson fired back: "Why don't you hang the Radical Republicans!"

As Johnson descended from the back of the balcony, supporters reminded him to ignore his hecklers and maintain his dignity. Johnson's replied: "I don't care about my dignity"—a quote that ran in the next day's newspapers across the country.

As Johnson was leaving the balcony, he was handed a folded note by one of his senior staff. The note read:

> Mr. President, I would seek the honor of a short audience with you tomorrow morning on the subject of the Freedmen's Bureau. It is urgent. I have left my contact information with your staff.
>
> Yours,
>
> General Oliver Otis Howard,
> Commissioner, Freedman's Bureau

President Johnson knew General Howard well: a career U.S. Army officer, Union General in the War. He had gone to Bowdoin College, and earned a commission at West Point. He lost his right arm at the Battle of Fair Oaks four years ago. He fought at Chancellorsville and Gettysburg. In 1865, he was given charge of the Freedman's Bureau as its first Commissioner. He was called the "Christian General" because during the Seminole Wars in Florida, he had experienced a conversion to evangelical Christianity. Johnson was told that Howard had considered resigning from the Army to become a minister—but had been talked out of it.

The President arranged to have General Howard summoned to his private hotel rooms the next morning, where the two had breakfast together.

As Howard stepped into the room, the President greeted him with ceremonial warmth.

"General, it is a pleasure to visit with you again. How is Elizabeth Anne, and your children?"

"All seven are well," Howard said, with a slight bow. "Thank you for asking."

"And what, pray, brings you to the city of Cleveland?" Johnson asked, motioning for the bearded General to join him at the small table for breakfast.

"You know, Mr. President, that my tenure at the Freedman's Bureau has been an important calling in my life…"

"Indeed," the President said.

"I said during the War that our mission is to destroy slavery—root and branch! This is a hard duty—a terrible, solemn duty---but it is a duty."

"And many thank you for this zeal."

"You may know that I was sent west to join General Sherman on his March to the Sea, and I witnessed the Fall of Atlanta."

"A decisive turning point in the War," Johnson added.

"During that campaign I saw first-hand the enormous suffering of the negro population," Howard said. "Unimaginable deprivation and suffering…Last May, I was called to Washington and asked to lead the Bureau of Refugees, Freedmen, and Abandoned Lands, to provide humanitarian relief for the South and to shepherd those four million people you mentioned in your speech last night, from slavery to citizenship. For me, this was a new experiment in governing. Frankly, Mr. President, I saw this opportunity as Heaven sent. I embraced the cause of the freed people as the mission that would guide the rest of my life."

Johnson poured tea for General Howard, and for himself.

"I was not long in office," Howard admitted, "when I realized that our government had little capacity to change white Southerners. These men were still fighting the Civil War. I am a military man by background and training. I do not have the political and administrative skills to implement land redistribution policies that will change the economic, social, and political dynamics of the South. I have therefore, as Commissioner, focused my energies on improving education for the freedmen, which is the true relief from beggary and dependence. Even now, I am working on a plan to open a new institution for higher education for black men and woman in the Nation's Capital—almost in the shadow of the White House."

Johnson turned in his chair to face General Howard directly.

"General—and I hope you will not receive these comments on a personal level---I have made no secret of my unhappiness with the Freedman's Bureau. As you heard me mention last night, I was opposed to the Freedmen's Bill, and opposed to pouring another $12 million into its activities in the South. I opposed the premise upon which the First Reconstruction Act was based - that there were no lawful governments in the seceded states. I vetoed the bill, but Congress wasted no time overriding my veto by 135 to 48 in the House and 38 to 10 in the Senate."

"You know me, General Howard," Johnson said. "You know that I ascended to this position upon the death of a man who was both venerated and despised. I rose from the tailor's bench to the Presidency. Like our Savior, Jesus Christ, I am willing to pardon repentant sinners. But Congress, in the person of the Republican Radicals, want to break up the Union—something which I believe neither you nor I want."

Johnson waited for Howard to respond. Seeing no pushback, he continued.

"Did you know that Radical Republicans have called my Swing Circle trip 'the remarkable circus that traveled through the country, and cut outside the circle and entered into street brawls with common blackguards?' While you are trying to do your job at the Freedman's Bureau, the Radical Republicans are spreading rumors that I have been drunk at several of my recent appearances. They called me a 'vulgar, drunken demagogue who was disgracing the presidency.'-They are crucifying me, General Howard."

"Mr. President, the most vulgar behavior I have seen in my life is what we have inflicted as a nation--and continue to inflict---on millions of freedmen in the South. The Northern missionary and aid societies have worked in conjunction with the Freedmen's Bureau to provide education for former slaves. We have helped establish eleven colleges in southern states for the education of freedmen. The primary focus of these groups was to raise funds to pay teachers and manage schools—"

Johnson extended his right arm, palm raised, towards Howard's chest.

70

"Let me stop you there, General," Johnson said. "The military rule which the First Reconstruction Act establishes is not to be used for any purpose of order or for the prevention of crime--but solely as a means of coercing the people into the adoption of principles and measures to which they are opposed. The power given to the commanding officer over all the people of each district is that of an absolute monarch. His mere will is to take the place of all law. He alone is permitted to determine what are rights of person or property. It places at his free disposal all the lands and goods in his district. Being bound by no State law, he may make a criminal code of his own; and he can make it as bloody as any recorded in history."

"Everything is a crime which he chooses to call so, and all persons are condemned whom he pronounces to be guilty. He may arrest his victims wherever he finds them, without warrant, accusation, or proof of probable cause. It is plain that the authority here given to the military officer amounts to absolute despotism. It reduces the whole population of the ten States--all persons, of every color, sex, and condition, and every stranger within their limits--to the most abject and degrading slavery. No master ever had a control so absolute over the slaves as this bill gives to the military officers over both white and colored persons."

Johnson took a quick sip of tea and put down his cup.

"The purpose and object of the bill is to change the entire structure and character of the State governments and to compel them by force to the adoption of laws and regulations. The negroes have not asked for the privilege of voting. The vast majority of them have no idea what it means. This bill not only thrusts it into their hands, but compels them, as well as the whites, to use it in a particular way. This bill imposes the Africanizing of the southern part of our territory. To force the right of suffrage out of the hands of the white people and into the hands of the negroes is an arbitrary violation of this principle."

At this point, General Howard rose to his feet.

"Mr. President let me speak plainly. You intend to stand for election as President in 1868. You no longer have the grace and dignity of Mr. Lincoln by your side, rest his soul. You seek a coalition of Democrats and Moderate Republicans. But if you continue to spurn the efforts of the Freedmen's Bureau and Reconstruction generally, if you continue to deny the negro the right to vote---I believe you will most assuredly not prevail maintaining your present office. I came here today because of the hatred I heard you announce last night. In good faith I implore you to embrace a compromise— to extend the work of the Freedmen's Bureau, to find middle ground on Reconstruction, and to lift up the former slave. Because if you fail to lift up the slave, you will sink down yourself, and your political aspirations will be beyond your reach!"

"If that be true," Johnson said with finality, "and I sink down, then the rest of America will sink down with me. Remember General, the Radical Republicans, with whom you conspire, have dismissed me as a vulgar, drunken demagogue---a disgrace to the presidency. I have nothing to lose with these people by continuing to act in such a manner. We shall learn in 1868 who the American people consider vulgar and drunken."

"Let me be so bold," Howard said, "as to predict that you, Sir, shall not celebrate a victory this November, and that the Freedman's Bureau will outlive your days in political office!"

Johnson held out his hand to General Howard, who came to formal attention, shook Johnson's hand once, briskly, turned on his heels, and left the President to his thoughts.

Post Script:

Congress passed the Freedmen's Bureau Act two times, and President Johnson vetoed it twice. But on the second time, Congress overrode the veto. Preparing for his next political run, Johnson called for a convention of the National Union Party, hoping to use the party name that had worked so well to elect Lincoln and Johnson. But in the mid-term election of 1866, the Republicans won by a landslide, gaining a two-thirds majority in Congress. Johnson complained that his Democrats had failed to rally in support of the National Union movement.

In the summer of 1867, Congress passed a Reconstruction Act. President Johnson vetoed it, but Congress overrode him again, and then adjourned. The new law deprived the President of control over the Army in the South. The President then issued a proclamation pardoning most Confederates. The Republicans were deeply angered by these actions. Johnson invoked more ire when he fired his Secretary of War, Edward Stanton, who refused to resign. The House impeached the President for intentionally violating the Tenure of Office Act, which said that a President could not remove certain office-holders without approval of the Senate. Johnson was put through a three-month impeachment trial in the spring of 1868. Johnson was advised by his supporters never to attend the trial, and to make no public comments about the charges.

Johnson managed to gain an acquittal, but at the 1868 Democratic National Convention in New York, he became a sitting President who was unable to gain the nomination of his party. By the 22nd ballot, he received only 4 votes—all from his home state of Tennessee.

But this was not the end of Johnson's political career. Seven years later, after several unsuccessful efforts to run for Congress from Tennessee, a Senate seat came open in 1875, and on the 54th ballot, by one vote, Johnson became the first former President to be elected to the Senate.

He served in one short Senate session, and while home in Tennessee during the break, suffered a stroke and died at the age of 66.

General Oliver Otis Howard was unable to get Johnson to support the Freedman's Bureau, but he had the full support of the Radical Republicans, who took over control of Congress in the 1866 elections. Howard remained as Commissioner of the Freedman's Bureau for another 8 years. He oversaw efforts to integrate freed slaves into the larger society, and sponsoring social programs, schools, courts, and medical care for the freedmen.

Howard promoted higher education for freedmen, including the founding of Howard University in the nation's capital, and serving at President of that institution for six years.

In his later years, General Howard's career took a very different course. He was ordered to command troops in the American West, leading military actions against many Native American tribes. After the controversial Indian Wars, Howard was named superintendent of West Point Military Academy for two years and served in other military commands. He retired from the Army in 1894 after 40 years of service.

He was awarded the Legion of Honor by the French government in 1884 and died in Vermont in 1909 at the age of 78.

EVER HEARD OF KARL MARX?

There was a crush of reporters and the popping of flash bulbs filling up Hearing Room 357 for the second day of testimony at the Army Signal Corps Subversion and Espionage Hearings on the morning of March 11, 1954.

The session was gaveled to order by the Republican Chairman of the Senate Operations Committee, also the Chair of the Permanent Subcommittee on Investigations: Senator Joseph R. McCarthy of Wisconsin.

Seated at the witness table in front of a collage of microphones was a black woman, Mrs. Annie Lee Moss, wearing a light-colored overcoat with a fur collar and a velour hat. Moss was bundled up as if she was still outside in the brisk March D.C. air. She appeared slumped down in her coat in anticipation of the hammering she has expected to receive from the Subcommittee. Sitting to her right was Mr. George F.C. Hayes, her attorney.

Moss looked out directly at the panel of six Senators, in addition to Chairman McCarthy, who would be asking her questions. On the Democratic side, were Senators Stuart Symington of Missouri, Henry M. Jackson of Washington, and John L. McClellan of Arkansas. Behind Senator McCarthy was his Chief Counsel, Roy M. Cohn, and behind Senator Jackson was the Chief Counsel for the Minority---29-year old Robert F. Kennedy.

"You are not here because you were considered important in the Communist apparatus," Chairman McCarthy told witness Moss. "We have the testimony that you are, or have been, a Communist. We are rather curious, though, to know how someone like yourself, who is known to your superiors to have a Communist record, how you suddenly were shifted from a worker in a cafeteria to the code room? I am today much more interested in the handling of your case by your superiors than in your own personal activities.

Counsel Roy Cohn then asked Moss, "While in the Pentagon, since 1950, have you had any connection with coded messages? Have you ever handled coded messages?"

"No more than to transmit the messages," Moss answered. "Receive or to transmit messages was all I had to do. I have never been in the code room in my life."

"And were some of those coded messages classified." Cohn asked.

"Well, I assume they were coded messages, classified messages coded."

"And you continued doing that work until some short time ago?"

"Yes. That is right," Moss replied.

"Around the period of time you were called before the committee, they changed you over to the supply room, is that right?

"That is right."

"And after the committee held some hearings you were suspended?"

"That is right."

"Going back to 1942 and 1943: The committee has had testimony that you were at that time a member of the Northeast Club of the Communist Party. Is that testimony true?"

"No, sir," answered Moss, leaning closer to the microphone. "It is not. Not at any time have I been a member of a Communist Party and I have never seen a Communist card."

"Have you ever attended any Communist meetings?"

"No, sir. I have never attended any Communist meetings."

"Have you ever subscribed to the *Daily Worker*?" Cohn asked.

"No, sir. I didn't subscribe to the *Daily Worker* and I wouldn't pay for it."

At this point, Chairman McCarthy asked the photographers to stop using flashbulbs, and to remove themselves from between the Committee and its witness.

Then McCarthy asked Moss about the statement from an FBI agent.

"Mrs. Markward, who was working for the FBI---who joined the Communist Party under orders from the FBI---has testified that while she never met you personally at a Communist Party meeting, that your name was on the list of Communists who were paying dues. Can you shed any light upon that?"

"No, sir. I do not even know what the dues are or where they were paid," Moss stated.

"With reference to your testimony about the *Daily Worker*," Cohn continued, "isn't it a fact that you regularly received the *Daily Worker* and that you arranged to receive it through Rob Hall, who was one of the leading Communists in the District of Columbia?"

"Rob Hall brought that paper to my house, where I was rooming, one Sunday morning, and my son tells me that my husband told him not to bring that paper back there anymore. And he said he paid him for whatever he had, and he didn't bring it anymore, and we didn't get this Communist paper any more until after we had moved southwest, at 72 R Street."

McCarthy asked: "Did you know Robert Hall?"

"No, sir, not personally."

"Do you know what business Robert Hall had with your husband besides merely delivering the copy of the *Daily Worker*?

"No, sir, I do not."

At this point, Senator McCarthy gathered up some of his papers and rose abruptly from his seat. "I am afraid I am going to have to excuse myself. I have a rather important appointment tonight which I have to work on right now."

McCarthy asked his ranking Republican Senator, Karl Mundt of North Dakota, to take over conduct of the hearing.

Mundt asked Moss if she knew what business Robert Hall had with her husband?

"I didn't remember the man's name until my son reminded we who he was. I had to ask him what was the man's name? But I didn't even remember his name. I remember seeing a Robert Hall around the union hall where we went to our union meetings, and I presumed he was the same man."

Senator Mundt then tried to establish if Robert Hall was a black man or a white man. He asked Moss if the man who came to her house to collect money for the *Daily Worker* newspaper was black or white?

"That was a white gentleman," Moss said.

"Is Mr. Hall a colored gentleman?" Mundt sought to clarify.

"This was a white gentleman who came to collect." Moss asserted.

"I understand," Mundt said. "But is Mr. Hall a colored gentleman?"

"Yes. The one whom I saw was colored."

Counsel Cohn then changed the topic to the newspaper again.

"You knew the *Daily Worker* was a Communist paper, did you not?"

"No, sir. Sure didn't."

"Well, when you read it, wasn't it pretty clear to you?"

"I didn't read it," Moss insisted, "because I don't read any newspaper very much."

"Did Robert Hall ever talk to you about the *Daily Worker*?"

"No, sir. Because I only saw Robert Hall around that union place."

"Isn't it a fact that when you testified before the House Committee on Un-American Activities in executive session you said under oath that Robert Hall had talked to you about the *Daily Worker* and told you it was a good paper?"

"No, sir; I have no knowledge of that. The man who came to collect told me it was a good paper."

Senator Symington then joined the conversation, directing his comment towards Senate Mundt, who was still chairing the hearing.

"Mr. Chairman," Symington asked, "I do not know what the importance of the fact whether or not the *Daily Worker* was or was not read is. Is the purpose to show that the *Daily Worker*, if you read it, that you are subversive?"

Counsel Cohn then explained his line of questioning: "Senator, what we are trying to bring out is this: First of all, Robert Hall was one of the three top Communists in the Communist Party of the District of Columbia. We felt there was significance to the fact that Robert Hall had come to the home of Mrs. Moss and persuaded her or somebody in her house to subscribe to the *Daily Worker*. Furthermore, there is a direct conflict in the testimony here this afternoon and the testimony before the House Committee on Un-American Activities where she stated that Hall described to her that the *Daily Worker* was a good paper."

"May I suggest that she be asked how many times she ever saw Mr. Hall?" Senator Symington responded.

Mundt asked Moss how often she met Hall. Moss said there were union meetings once a month—but she didn't go to all of them.

Mundt then asked Moss directly: "Did you know that Mr. Hall was a Communist?"

"No, sir. I never had heard of communism until 1948 when this first hearing came up, and I asked them then what was that?"

Under questioning from Democratic Senator Jackson, Moss explained that she was a member of the cafeteria workers union. She said she had grown up in South Carolina, had moved to North Carolina, and never finished high school.

Jackson asked if Moss had ever been asked to join the Communist party?

"I don't know," Moss replied. "This union — I don't know whether it was Communist or not-- all I know is that they took our dues out before our checks were issued."

Counsel Robert Kennedy signaled Senator Jackson that he had a question to ask Mrs. Moss.

"Did you say. Mrs. Moss, you knew Rob Hall or did you not know Rob Hall?

"I didn't know him personally. I wasn't a personal friend of his. I saw him around the union hall."

"But you never met him personally?"

"I guess I have spoke to him," Moss said, "but he wasn't a personal friend of mine."

"Was he the one who brought the *Daily Workers* to your home, or was that somebody else?"

"My son said it was somebody else." Moss replied.

"Was it Mr. Hall?" Kennedy asked.

"Yes."

"Did he signify it was the same Mr. Hall that you saw around the union hall?"

" Well, now, I don't know," Moss said.

"Did you feel at that time it was the same?"

"I felt it was the same man," Moss said.

"...Who came and collected the money at a later date?" Kennedy continued.

"This was a white gentleman who came to collect the money," Moss said.

Kennedy paused, scribbling a few notes. He looked up again. "Was Mr. Hall a colored gentleman, or..."

"Yes, sir."

Kennedy put down his pencil. "There is some confusion about it, is there not, Mr. Cohn? Is the Rob Hall we are talking about--the union organizer-- was he a white man or colored man"?

Cohn leaned into the microphone: "I never inquired into his race. I am not sure. We can check that, though. My assumption has been that he is a white man, but we can check that.

Senator Symington circled back to the witness. "The Bob Hall that you knew--does he look like a colored man or does he look more like a white man."

"He was colored, the one I knew of. The man I have in mind as Robert Hall was a man about my complexion."

"Let's decide which Robert Hall we want to talk about," said a frustrated Symington.

Kennedy then asked Moss again: "When you spoke about the union organizer, you spoke about Rob Hall, and I think we all felt that was the colored gentleman?"

Cohn shot a look over at Kennedy, then added: "I was not talking about a union organizer, Bob. I was talking about a Communist organizer who at that time, according to the public record, was in charge of subscriptions for the *Daily Worker* in the District of Columbia area.

"Evidently," Kennedy said slowly, "it is a different Rob Hall."

"I don't know that it is." Cohn shot back. "Our information is that it was the same Rob Hall.

Senator McClellan jumped in: "If one is black, and the other is white, there is a difference."

"I think that might better be something we should go into and get some more exact information on," Cohn concluded.

"I think so, too," Kennedy demurred.

As Moss' testimony neared its conclusion, Senator McClellan of Arkansas asked Moss to explain what she did to "transmit messages." "I would like to know a little about the position, the nature of your work, exactly what you do. I see you only get a salary of about $3,300 a year, which is a very low salary, I think, for any responsible position."

Moss explained that in the beginning she had to "route" some messages.

"Did that require any knowledge of what the message contained?" McClellan asked.

"No, sir."

"Did you have time to decipher?"

"No, sir."

"It was simply as a matter of routine, a mechanical process after they were received, getting them moving to their proper destination?" McClellan asked.

"That is right."

"And that is all you did?"

"Yes, sir, that is all."

McClellan then told the Committee: "While I am opposed to any Communist being in Government, it has not been established to my satisfaction that this woman is a Communist."

Senator Symington asked Moss what she was doing now, was she working?

"No, sir," Moss admitted.

"Why not?" Symington inquired.

"I was suspended...by the Department of the Army. Until this is over."

"What reason did they give for suspending you?"

"The immediate suspension is deemed necessary," Moss read off the paper handed to her by her lawyer, "and advisable in the interest of national security under the authority of Public Law 733, 81st Congress, and Executive Order 10-450, pending adjudication of your case under AR 620-220-1."

Symington then asked: "Have you ever, to the best of your knowledge, have you ever talked to a Communist in your life?"

"No, sir, not to my knowledge."

"Did you ever heard of Karl Marx?"

"Who is that?" Moss asked.

"I will pass the question," Symington told the Chair,

"Do you think you are a good American?" Symington asked,

"Yes."

"Would you ever do anything to hurt your country?"

"No, sir."

"What are you living on now? Have you got any savings?"

"No, sir," Moss said.

"Do you need work?"

"Sure, I do."

"If you do not get work pretty soon, what are you going to do?"

"I am going down to the welfare."

In his final summary to the Committee, Roy Cohn told members:

"We have the testimony of Mrs. Markward, the undercover agent for the FBI, stating that an Annie Lee Moss was a member---a dues-paying member---of the Communist Party, the Northeast Club of the Communist Party. We have corroboration of that testimony by another witness who was called before the committee and gave a sworn statement to the effect that she also knew Mrs. Moss as a member of the Northeast Club of the Communist Party."

Senator McClellan then objected to Mr. Cohn's statement. "Mr. Chairman, I would like to make this point: We are making statements here against a witness who has come and submitted to cross-examination. She has already lost her job. She has been suspended because of this action. I am not defending her. If she is a Communist, I want her exposed. But to make these statements that we have corroborating evidence that she is a Communist, under these circumstances, I think she is entitled to have it produced here in her presence and let the public know about it and let her know about it. So, I move that the evidence be produced. I do not like to try people by hearsay evidence. I want to get the testimony under oath."

Chairman Mundt then ruled that Mr. Cohn's comment be stricken from the record. "I think we better take it up in executive session, whether we should try to produce a witness in public, because the FBI may have her under cover."

Symington pressed on with his point. "I think the record ought to show that Mrs. Markward says that she has never seen Mrs. Annie Lee Moss at any Communist meeting. Mrs. Markward has testified that Annie Lee Moss was registered with the Communist Party in 1943 and later her name was shifted over to the Communist Political Association of Washington for 1944. Mrs. Markward cannot recall ever having seen Mrs. Annie Lee Moss at any Communist Party meeting, but it is her recollection that Mrs. Moss paid her dues and was a member in good standing."

Symington then turned back to Moss.

"Isn't it possible," the Senator asked, "that there are some other people named Moss, just like apparently there are some other people named Hall?"

"Yes, sir. That is true." Moss said.

"Do you know anybody else in this town named Moss? Have you ever looked up a telephone number — are there any Mosses in Washington besides you?

"Yes, sir. There are three Annie Lee Mosses," she answered.

Spontaneous laughter darted around the hearing room.

Symington then thanked Mrs. Moss for her testimony, and closed with this: "Mrs. Moss, I want to say something to you, and I may be sticking my neck out and I may be wrong. But I have been listening to you testify this afternoon, and I think you are telling the truth. If you are not taken back into the Army, you come around and see me, and I am going to see that you get a job."

About a week after the hearing closed, the Chief Counsel for the Democrats drove over to Mrs. Moss' house to pay her a visit.

Mrs. Moss, at first quite surprised, made Kennedy some coffee, and a few store-bought cookies, and sat down in her small living room in the thinning afternoon light.

"Mrs. Moss," Robert Kennedy said, "I just wanted to tell you on behalf of the Senate members I represent, that your testimony before the Senate committee last week was inspiring. I had to restrain myself when you said there were three other Annie Lee Mosses in the Washington, D.C. phone book! And you had them turning circles over Rob Hall the white man versus Rob Hall the black man. I believe that Chairman McCarthy got up to leave the hearing suddenly because it was going so badly for the Republicans."

Moss said she had wondered why Joe McCarthy had just packed up in the middle of the hearing and left. "I didn't know if something I said had offended him," Moss wondered. "It seemed like a sudden decision to leave..."

"I also want to apologize for the rough treatment you have received at the hands of the Army," Kennedy said, "and I encourage you to take up Senator Symington's offer to help you find work."

"Thank you, Mr. Kennedy," Moss said. "My family deeply appreciates the help you gave us at the hearing. I was so nervous I was not sure I could finish it."

"I tried to get some of your records from the FBI, but I think I made a few enemies over there in the process."

"Mr. Kennedy, "those HUAC people are crazy. What they're doing to this country is just crazy."

"Some of them mean well," Kennedy said. "This is just a bad period we need to see through with the least damage possible."

"What happens now---if I may ask?" Moss said.

"I don't think the Committee is going to push any further with your case," Kennedy assured her. "I think they run the risk of looking like a bully if they try to press the issue."

"I don't think I could go through that again---so I hope this is the end of it."

"Mrs. Moss," Kennedy smiled, "I will be watching Roy Cohn and his staff every minute. If anything more has to happen, you will hear from me personally."

As Kennedy was opening the screen door to leave Moss' home, she held out her hand to shake his. "Can I tell you something personal?" she asked.

"Of course," Kennedy said, holding onto the handshake.

"I have never once had a white man pay me a visit in my home."

"Well," Kennedy said, flashing a wide smile. "I'm honored to be the first."

Moss held onto Kennedy's hand.

"One more thing, Mr. Kennedy," she said. "My son tells me I should have known who that comedy man Marx was. He says he's seen all his movies on TV."

Post Script:

When Annie Lee Moss was called to testify before the House of Un-American Activities Committee, she was suspended from her job with the Army Signal Corps. Within a week after the hearing, film footage of Moss' testimony was broadcast on Edward R. Murrow's popular TV show See It Now. *Murrow called the segment "a little picture about a little woman."*

Roughly ten months after her appearance before the HUAC, Moss was rehired by the Army's Finance and Accounts Office, where she worked as an Army clerk for twenty years until she retired. Annie Lee Moss died in 1996 in Washington, D.C. at the age of 90.

When Democrats gained the majority of seats in the Senate in 1955, Robert F. Kennedy became the Chief Majority Counsel for the U.S. Senate Permanent Subcommittee on Investigations. In the 1956 presidential election, Kennedy worked as an aide for Democratic candidate Adlai Stevenson.

In 1959, Robert Kennedy ran his brother Jack's presidential campaign. After Jack Kennedy won the 1960 presidential election, he appointed his younger brother Robert to serve as Attorney General.

In August,1964, nine months after his brother's assassination, Robert Kennedy left the Executive Branch and announced his candidacy for a seat in the U.S. Senate representing the state of New York. After winning his election, one of the issues Kennedy advocated for was gun control. In May, 1965 he co-sponsored legislation to put federal restrictions on mail-order gun sales. Kennedy said he wanted to keep firearms away from "people who have no business with guns or rifles...the very young, those with criminal records and the insane." Congress ultimately passed the Gun Control Act in 1968.

Kennedy declared his candidacy for the Presidency in March, 1968. But three months later, at the age of 42, he was shot and killed in Los Angeles while campaigning by a 24 year-old gunman carrying a revolver.

BEAST OF VERMONT

"I find myself surrounded by felons, counterfeiters, thieves, and runaway slaves," laughed Matthew Lyon. "Not altogether that different than when I was seated in Congress."

Congressman Lyon, 49, sat on the edge of a small wooden bed in his 16' x 12' cell in Vergennes, Vermont. Facing him on a chair near the latrine was someone he knew only as "Byrd." Byrd, for some reason, had befriended Lyon during his incarceration, and managed to provide him with paper and writing materials, and an occasional bit of dried meat. For that, Lyon was grateful, no questions asked.

It was November, 1798, in the second month of Lyon's four-month sentence for Sedition against the United States Government. The Federalist controlled Congress, with support from President John Adams, had passed a series of four laws, the Alien and Seditions Acts, which gave the government the power to deport foreigners, and to make it more difficult for immigrants to vote. The Alien Act required an immigrant to live in America for 14 years before having the right to vote—nearly three times longer than previous law. One Federalist declared his purpose to stop "hordes of Wild Irishmen" and the "turbulent and disorderly of all the world" from coming to America "with a basic view to distract our tranquility." The legislative package also authorized the President to deport aliens, and permit their arrest, imprisonment, and deportation during wartime.

Even more controversial was The Sedition Act. The Federalists believed that America was on the precipice of war with France. The opposition party in Congress, the Democratic-Republicans, were viewed as French sympathizers who were disloyal to the nation. The Sedition Act made it a crime for American citizens to "print, utter, or publish . . . any false, scandalous, and malicious writing" about the U.S. Government. The laws seemed to be politically targeted: the only journalists prosecuted under the Sedition Act were editors of Democratic-Republican newspapers. Matthew Lyon, a Democratic-Republican congressman from Vermont was the first person to be charged under the Sedition Act for an essay he wrote in *Spooner's Vermont Journal* accusing President Adams of "ridiculous pomp, foolish adulation, and selfish avarice."

Lyon himself had predicted that "very likely" he would be the first person to be tried under the Sedition Act. He was correct. He said publicly that he did not believe in the "principle of Presidential infallibility."

At the sentencing, Federalist Judge George Patterson said he wanted to make an example of Lyon, who was a Republican, and held high public office. The Judge lamented that he was unable to render a harsher punishment. But he specifically insisted that Lyon be given nothing to read, and nothing with which to write, during his internment.

When Lyon arrived under guard at the jail in Vergennes, he found a cold stone room with no glass in the single small window of his cell, and no stove. He had to wear his long coat all day, and had no comforter to shelter him from the deepening Vermont winter.

"The French Revolution was the powder keg which blew apart the Federalists from the Republicans," Lyon told his visitor Byrd. "The Federalists viewed the Revolution--and the French Council of 500--as mob rule, while the Republicans applauded the overthrow of the French aristocratic class."

"But it has been rumored that Talleyrand is plotting an invasion of America," Byrd responded. "And they point to the undeclared Quasi War in the Caribbean as proof!"

"What did we expect?" Lyon objected. "Our nation told the French Republic that we would stop repaying our debt—because it was owed to a previous government. French privateers begin seizing our ships trading with Britain. I do not blame them: these ships are prizes to be ransomed!"

"But in the past year," Byrd argued, "we are told that the French have seized 316 American merchant ships!"

"And we have been attacking their ships..." Lyon answered. "It is all scripted. Last May, Congress annulled the Treaty of Alliance, and two days later we were boarding French warships."

"And do you not blame Foreign Minister Talleyrand for this affair?" Byrd wondered.

"It is our President who begins preparations for war. Do you recall his words last spring to Congress? He said that France sought to 'produce divisions fatal to our peace,' and said we should repel France, and show the world that 'we are not a degraded people, humiliated under a colonial spirit of fear and sense of inferiority, fitted to be the miserable instruments of foreign influence.' No wonder the French Directory is on edge!"

"And you believe what came to pass at your sedition trial as evolving from this conflict?" Byrd asked.

"I do," Lyon insisted. "It is a direct line of causality. Although Adams was not the framer of the Sedition Act, he supported it fully. The President believed that journalists who deliberately distort the news to mislead the people would produce great harm in our representative democracy. The Federalists found a warning letter outside the President's residence— concerning a French plot to set fire to Philadelphia and massacre its residents. They summoned hundreds of militiamen to patrol the city's streets, with a special guard around Adam's home. The President ordered 'chests of arms from the war office to defend my house at the expense of my life.' No wonder my friend Benjamin Bache calls the President 'old, querulous, bald, blind, crippled, and toothless Adams.'"

Byrd shifted his weight in his chair and wagged a pointed finger back at Lyon. "And they call you a 'mobocrat.' Noah Webster says you Republicans are 'the refuse, the sweepings of the most depraved part of mankind from the most corrupt nations on earth.'"

"He is too kind," Lyon mocked the comment. "The Federalists are deeply troubled by our nation's rapidly growing immigrant population. One newspaper has labeled them 'none but the most vile and worthless.' The President's own nephew, Mr. Shaw, claims that all our present difficulties may be traced to the hordes of Foreigners. He counsels that America should no longer be 'an asylum to all nations.'

"You are aware," Byrd interjected, "that the Federalists call you 'the Beast of Vermont' because of your altercation on the floor of the House earlier this year?"

"Nine months ago," Lyon jumped in, "I was involved in an unfortunate incident with the Federalist Roger Griswold. The Congressman called me a scoundrel. When I said I was prepared to fight for the interest of the common man, Griswold mocked me with an incident many years ago when I was under General Gates' command. I spat tobacco juice on Griswold—and for that conduct, I was labeled this 'Beast' you refer to---and called the 'Spitting Irishman.'"

"Not an admirable title for a Congressman," Byrd responded.

"But I apologized later to the entire House. I did not know we were in session when I responded to Mr. Griswold's insults. I meant no breach of decorum or disrespect to the Members. But two weeks later, Griswold attacked me with a wooden cane, beating me about the head and shoulders in full view of other Representatives on the House floor. I had no recourse but to defend myself until the conflict was broken up. They had to drag Mr. Griswold by the legs to get him to relinquish his grip. Griswold and I were later censured, but the House refused to vote on any motion, so the issue died. We both promised that we would remain on good behavior. I, however, have been unable to outrun the 'Beast' that was placed on my shoulders."

Lyon rose to his feet and walked over to the small open window in his cell, which looked out beyond its bars into a hallway about four stones wide, across from another cell. In the first week of his sentence, Lyon had counted 36 stones to the end of his line of vision. "Do you have any tobacco?" he asked Byrd.

"Sorry, no," Byrd replied. Lyon kept pacing as he continued.

"Federalists say they are worried about the 60,000 Irish immigrants in the new nation, some of whom were exiled for plotting against British rule. Is it not ironic that plotting against British rule is what created America? I myself was born in County Wicklow, Ireland. When I was 14, I began learning the printing and bookkeeping trade. I came to Connecticut in 1764 as a redemptioner. To pay off my debt, I worked for a farmer and merchant in Woodbury, who sold my debt to another farmer in Litchfield."

"You came to America an absolute pauper?" Byrd said.

"Yes. But by working for wages when I could, I saved enough to buy out my indenture, and became a free man in 1768. During the Revolution, I served under Horatio Gates, and rose to the rank of Captain in Warner's regiment. I fought in Bennington and Saratoga. I became Colonel and paymaster general of the Vermont Militia. Eleven years after becoming a free man, I was elected to serve in the Vermont House of Representatives for four years, and founded the town of Fair Haven, Vermont, serving another thirteen years in the State House. I won election to Congress as a

Democratic-Republican in the 5th and 6th Congresses. From indentured servant to Congress in 33 years…"

"A remarkable feat at that!" Byrd added.

Lyon sat down, put both his hand on his knees, and stared full face into the face of Mr. Byrd. "Does that," Lyon said through his teeth, "sound to you like the profile of a seditionist?"

"So how did it proceed at your trial?" Byrd asked, looking for a safer haven for his conversation.

"The U.S. Supreme Court Justice William Paterson presided in the US circuit court for the District of Vermont. He was a Federalist appointed by John Adams---so you will know my fate in advance from this fact," Lyon said.

"Paterson told the jury that I was charged with seditious libel---which is a crime against the people who had elected government officials. The Grand Jury publicly thanked Paterson personally for his remarks, and the Jury agreed that domestic licentiousness was a greater threat than a host of invading foes."

"The Jury ate from his hand," Byrd commented.

"The Grand Jury declared I was a 'malicious and seditious person and of a depraved mind and wicked and diabolical disposition.' They said I had 'deceitfully, wickedly and maliciously' contrived to defame the government of the United States with intent and design to defame the government and John Adams the President, and to bring both into contempt and disrepute in order to excite against the said Government and President the hatred of the good people of the United States and to stir up sedition in the United States."

"But surely they enumerated specific grievances against you?" Byrd asked.

"They enumerated three counts against me: The first count of the indictment cited a published letter I wrote before the passage of the Sedition Act. I saw in the actions of the Executive Branch 'every consideration of the public welfare swallowed up in a continual grasp for power, in an unbounded thirst for ridiculous pomp, foolish adulations, and selfish avarice."

"The two other counts against me charged that I promoted sedition by publicizing a letter in which the poet Joel Barlow blamed Adams and the Senate for the diplomatic crisis with France and suggested that the President should be relegated to a mad-house."

"And what was your defense?" Byrd asked. "Who represented you before the Jury?"

"I presented my own defense," Lyon replied, "which lasted about two hours. I argued that none of my actions amounted to anything more than a legitimate opposition. I told the Jury that the Sedition Act—which I had voted against on the floor of the House—was unconstitutional, and I had demonstrated no intent to undermine the government."

"Even if the Act were constitutional, it would be unconstitutional for the court to apply the act to writings which were composed before the passage of the act. I stated that I did not intend to defame the President or the government. I noted that the contents of the publications were all true, and thus they could not be in violation of the Sedition Act."

"I called only one witness for my defense: Justice Paterson. To prove the truth of my statements regarding the President, I asked Paterson if he had, in fact, observed ridiculous pomp and parade when he dined at the Adams residence in Philadelphia."

"How did the Justice respond to that!" Byrd laughed.

"Paterson said 'No,' but he would not respond when I asked him if the President's house displayed more pomp and circumstances than at a neighborhood tavern in Rutland, Vermont, in my District?"

"Paterson instructed the jury that their deliberations had nothing whatever to do with the constitutionality or unconstitutionality of the Sedition law, and that they should only determine if I had actually published the letters and if my intent was to stir up sedition. The Justice said my publication of the letter was certain, so the jury had only to focus on whether my purpose was seditious."

"And..." Byrd said with some impatience. "What did the jury say?"

"Know you by my presence in this filthy sty of a cell what the outcome was. In less than one hour, the jury returned with a guilty verdict. Paterson said a

Member of Congress deserved severe punishment of four months in prison, and a $1,000 fine. He denied me even paper and pen---which through your kind auspices---I now have."

"And what of you now? Where lies your future course?" Byrd inquired.

"First, I plan to seek reelection to my seat, and to return to Philadelphia. I will live to see Adams' back as he walks out of office. I will cast my lot with Thom Jefferson and the Democratic-Republicans, and vote for repeal of the Sedition Act."

"And beyond that?"

"Beyond that, I am not sure. I have some family in Kentucky—but first I will finish my work in the Green Mountain state."

"How do you respond to those who say you should seek to be pardoned for your conviction?"

"I cannot be pardoned of an offense which I have not committed."

"But as it stands," Byrd continued, "you have been convicted of committing a most grave offense against the Nation."

"I seek no pardon from the Federalists—or their President," Lyon stated. "Did you know that the Allan Brothers—the Green Mountain Boys---offered to burn down this prison and set me free. But I told them to lay aside such plans. My retribution, I assured them, will come in 1800 when we elect Mr. Jefferson as our next President."

With that, Byrd got up first. He seemed agitated by the course of the conversation. He motioned to the pad of paper on Lyon's bed, and said: "Let me know when you need your supply of paper and pen refreshed. And let me know if you are ever feeling contrite about the events that led you to Vergennes."

"Mr. Byrd," Lyon replied, "you have extended a kindness to me in hearing my 'seditious' tale, and for carrying messages from this cell on my behalf. But I assure you, contrition is not on my lips now---or ever shall be."

Byrd promptly left Lyon in his cell without a parting handshake and went back to his office on the first level of the Vergennes prison. In his small office he opened a desk drawer and removed a pad of paper and a pen and composed a short note:

"Dear President Adams,

I have interviewed Mr. Lyon at length today, and he has assured me in conclusion that he has no contrition on his lips for what happened at his sedition trial.

I am more convinced than in earlier reports to you that this man remains a dangerous, imbalanced person who is obsessed by his hatred of all Federalists.

My firm recommendation to you, Mr. President, is that you not heed the calls of those who seek a pardon for Mr. Lyon. You will never get an apology from this man, and it will serve you little politically to seek one.

Best,

Mr. Byrd"

About two weeks later, an envelope arrived at the jail from the Office of the President in Philadelphia. Inside was a short note:

"Dear Mr. Byrd,

Penitence must precede pardon.

Thank you for your service,

John Adams"

Postscript:

After Thomas Jefferson was elected President in 1800, Matthew Lyon moved to Kentucky. He started a boat building company, which secured a contract to build gunboats for the U.S. Department of War during the War of 1812. The federal government never paid Lyon for his boats, and his company was forced into bankruptcy.

But Lyon was not finished with politics. He was elected to the Kentucky legislature, successfully representing his district in the U.S. Congress for 8 years, becoming the first American to serve in Congress from two different states.

Lyon was appointed by President James Monroe to work with the Cherokee Indians in the Arkansas Territories. Lyon ran again to serve as a delegate in Congress for the Territories. He lost by 61 votes in an election that he contested was rigged.

Matthew Lyon died in Arkansas in 1822. He was 73 years old.

I THOUGHT MY DAFFODILS WERE YELLOW

Winston Churchill was more than surprised—he was astonished---by what President Franklin Roosevelt announced to the press.

"The only terms on which we shall deal with an Axis government," Roosevelt told reporters, "or any Axis factions, are the terms proclaimed at this conference in Casablanca: 'Unconditional Surrender.' In our uncompromising policy we mean no harm to the common people of the Axis nations. But we do mean to impose punishment and retribution in full upon their guilty, barbaric leaders..."

It was the morning of January 24, 1943. Roosevelt and Churchill were holding a joint press conference on the lawn of the President's villa in Casablanca, Morocco. They were discussing the results from their top-secret Casablanca Conference which, for security reasons, had been covertly conducted over the past 10 days.

Wearing a white suit and no hat in the brilliant early sun, the President sat to the right of the Prime Minister, who wore a fedora, dark blue suit and bow tie, accented with a large starched white handkerchief inserted into his breast pocket, with his wooden walking stick propped against his chair. Both men sat in white wooden chairs framed by a backdrop of palm trees and bleached villas set on a hill overlooking the Atlantic Ocean.

Roosevelt had his long-stemmed cigarette holder, and Churchill was chewing on the end of an unlit, large cigar in his right hand. Behind them stood six of their U.S. and British Chiefs of Staff from the armed forces. Nearby was the three-story Anfa Hotel, which resembled a dry-docked cruise ship, upon which the United States, Great Britain and France has just spent nearly a week and a half in seclusion negotiating a strategy for the remainder of the war effort.

It had fallen to American General Dwight D. Eisenhower to make advance plans for the Casablanca Conference. Eisenhower reported back to the White House in December of 1942 that he had found a spot in Casablanca that was "top-rate"--- the Villa Mirado, which had a hotel nearby "surrounded by a group of excellent villas situated five miles south of Casablanca" which seemed ideal for the meeting. Eisenhower described the residence as "charming, exactly suited as to what was required," complete with a "nice garden, light and airy."

In Washington, the Secret Service picked up the luggage of U.S. officials traveling with Roosevelt at their homes, so that their travel plans would not be noticed at the White House or Pentagon. Roosevelt boarded a morning train on January 9th from the underground station at the Bureau of Engraving---not from Union Station---and headed north towards Baltimore, then turned back south to Florida. On January 11th, in Miami, Roosevelt and his delegation flew out on two Pan Am planes. This would be Roosevelt's fourth official meeting with Churchill. Casablanca was to be the first in a series of "mid-war" Allied conferences in the works. For the President, no other Commander-In-Chief had flown while in office, and no other President had left America in a time of war.

Arriving ahead of Roosevelt were General George Marshall, Chief of Staff of the United States Army, Navy Fleet Admiral Ernie King, and Air Force Lieutenant General Henry Arnold. They were all quartered at the Anfa Hotel with the other members of the Combined Chiefs of Staff.

Churchill reached Casablanca two days after Roosevelt. As part of Churchill's official entourage were Field Marshal Sir Alan Brooke, Chief of the Imperial General Staff, Admiral of the Fleet Sir Dudley Pound, First Sea Lord, and Air Chief Marshal Sir Charles F. A. Portal, Chief of the Air Staff. Helping to coordinate events was Field Marshal Sir John Dill, Chief of the British Joint Staff Mission in Washington.

The hotel and villas were surrounded by palm trees, bougainvillaea, and orange groves. The palm trees were protected by barbed wire entanglements, and the perimeter was patrolled by armed infantrymen and a large Secret Service delegation. Churchill's staff assembled a war room with the most current maps of the war fronts. The British and American leaders met over lunch and dinner tables, conducting informal discussions that lasted into the early morning. There were several plenary meetings and conferences for the Combined Chiefs of Staff. The French sent two generals to the conference: General Henri Giraud, High Commissioner of French Africa, and General Charles de Gaulle, leader of the Fighting French forces. Generalissimo Joseph Stalin was unable to attend the conference due to the pivotal situation unfolding in Stalingrad.

"I think we have all had it in our hearts and heads before," Roosevelt told the reporters, "but I don't think that it has ever been put down on paper by the Prime Minister and myself---and that is: the determination that peace can come to the world only by the total elimination of German and Japanese war power."

Roosevelt paused, and then told a story he knew Churchill would appreciate, as a lover of British and American history.

"Some of you Brits know this old story: We had a General called U. S. Grant. His name was Ulysses Simpson Grant, but in my---and the Prime Minister's--- early days---he was called 'Unconditional Surrender' Grant. In 1862, General Grant had captured Fort Donelson in Tennessee—a mere 10 days after taking Fort Henry. The Confederates tried to attack on the Union's right flank and center. Grant had to beat a retreat. But the Confederate General---over-confident that he could hold onto the Fort Donelson---pushed forward against the Union troops. Grant attacked the Confederate's right wing. The rebels had the Cumberland River at their rear. They attempted an escape--- but many of their troops were killed. When the Rebels asked for terms of surrender, General Grant told them: 'No terms will be accepted except unconditional and immediate surrender.'"

"The elimination of German, Japanese and Italian war power means the unconditional surrender by Germany, Italy, and Japan." Roosevelt noted. "That means a reasonable assurance of future world peace. I am not calling for the destruction of the peoples of Germany, Italy or Japan," FDR was careful to explain. "We will destroy the evil philosophies that these nations have chosen to pursue. We do mean to impose punishment and retribution in full upon their guilty, barbaric leaders."

Roosevelt privately told Churchill later that he had not planned on talking about unconditional surrender—but the subject had been broached during the Conference.

For his part, Churchill was not planning to announce such a policy---but he wanted to avoid any public disagreements that could undermine the war effort in the eyes of the public. He decided to stay on safe ground.

"I agree with everything the President has said," the Prime Minister affirmed. "One thing I should like to say, and that is: I think I can say it with full confidence—nothing that may occur in this war will ever come between me and the President. He and I are in this as friends and partners, and we work together. We know that our easy, free conversation is one of the sinews of war of the Allied Powers."

Although the Allied Forces had invested countless hours in Casablanca, many matters had been left on the table for future discussion. But the President felt strongly that a message needed to be sent to the Axis nations.

"The decisions reached and the actual plans made at Casablanca were not confined to any one theater of war or to any one continent or ocean or sea," Roosevelt told the press. "Before this year is out, it will be made known to the world--in actions rather than words--that the Casablanca Conference produced plenty of news; and it will be bad news for the Germans and Italians---and the Japanese."

Roosevelt stopped and pushed himself further up in his chair. His legs were crossed, and his coat jacket still buttoned.

"In an attempt to ward off the inevitable disaster," Roosevelt noted, "the Axis propagandists are trying all of their old tricks in order to divide the United Nations. They seek to create the idea that if we win this war, Russia, England, China, and the United States are going to get into a cat-and-dog fight. This is their final effort to turn one nation against another, in the vain hope that they may settle with one or two at a time--that any of us may be so gullible and so forgetful as to be duped into making 'deals' at the expense of our Allies. To these panicky attempts to escape the consequences of their crimes we say--all the United Nations say--that the only terms on which we shall deal with an Axis government or any Axis factions are the terms proclaimed at Casablanca: 'Unconditional Surrender.'"

"It is one of our war aims, as expressed in the Atlantic Charter, that the conquered populations of today be again the masters of their destiny. There must be no doubt anywhere that it is the unalterable purpose of the United Nations to restore to conquered peoples their sacred rights."

At the conclusion of the press conference, while their consolidated Chiefs of Staff were meeting in a plenary session at the Anfa hotel, Roosevelt and Churchill had agree to share a light meal together at the President's villa, after taking separate trips to review troops and installations in the city. They agreed that the meeting would be without staff.

The two world leaders lunched over a simple meal consisting of boiled ham, fruit salad, and coffee. Churchill was the first to speak:

"Franklin, you are looking well. How are you holding up?"

"About as well as could be expected after a 5,000 mile trip across the Atlantic," Roosevelt answered. "All the stealth and secrecy around these meetings does add a burden to the planning."

"Some of my own staff think I am still at Downing Street at this moment," Churchill laughed. "They are probably better off not having me there..."

Putting down his cup and lighting up a cigar, Churchill shifted to another topic on his mind.

"Franklin, may I have a few words in private here about your new Ambassador to the U.K.?"

"Certainly," Roosevelt answered. "I have heard good things about Ambassador Winant—I expect you've seen a significant change in approach than Joe Kennedy employed?"

"Yes, a very striking difference...When he first landed in Bristol—I think it was March of '41, Winant said: 'There is no place I'd rather be at this time than in England!' Good way to start the game, wouldn't you say?"

"John Winant was a great Governor in New Hampshire. He's a smart man..."

"Yes, quite so. He can be a bit moody at times, and I have been concerned about his emotional status and balance---but he is certainly a refreshing change from the pro-appeasement posture of Mr. J.P. Kennedy. You know, Winant was with me when I first got the news about Pearl Harbor... It was an awful mess when the Nazi's captured his son John, Jr. It drove the point home to the British public that Ambassador Winant's son was a bomber pilot who now was a prisoner of war. It earned him great sympathy across the isles. A great contrast to the lack of sympathy extended to the previous Ambassador, Mr. Kennedy."

"I must admit that I have been truly puzzled by some of Joe Kennedy's statements," Roosevelt said. "I brought Joe onboard as Ambassador in '38. It didn't take too long to see the cracks appear. Over the past year I was tempted on many occasions to recall him."

"Ambassador Kennedy was inclined to believe that we could make a deal with Herr Hitler," Churchill scoffed, raising an eyebrow. "I sometimes thought I was talking to Neville Chamberlain. Kennedy apparently suggested to my staff that he could arrange an audience with Hitler himself. Here we were, in the very teeth of the London bombing, and our U.S. Ambassador is talking about a rapprochement with Hitler! He wanted to reach a 'better understanding' between America and the Nazis. It bordered on delusional."

"Kennedy was dead-set against providing military or economic aid to the U.K.," Roosevelt added. "A lot of that anti-interventionist attitude was in the air. He was not alone in that opinion---but I can appreciate the uncomfortable position he placed you in."

"He reportedly told one of your newspapers that 'Democracy is finished in England,'" Churchill scoffed. "I wanted to cuff him with my cane. Kennedy told the press: 'I know more about the European situation than anybody else, and it's up to me to see that the country gets it.' This is not the stuff from which Diplomacy is made..."

"Kennedy told me before he left for London," Roosevelt confided, "that Britain was 'fighting for self-preservation, just as we Americans will if it comes to us...'"

"In London he was viewed as a staunch isolationist, a defeatist," Churchill admitted. "We were being bombed nightly. The Royal Family chose to stay in Buckingham Palace—yet Ambassador Kennedy retreats to his country estate! One member of my foreign office said 'I thought my daffodils were yellow, until I met Joe Kennedy.' The appearance was awful."

"Winston, all of this has been most awkward for me. You know I have relied heavily on Joe Kennedy for support with the Catholic voters. When I called the Ambassador back to the White House, aside from our differences over Britain, I asked him to do a nationwide radio speech in support of my re-election bid. He rallied the Irish Catholics for me. Shortly after the election, Joe resigned his ambassadorship—I did not have to ask him."

Churchill put down his cigar and inched his chair slightly closer to Roosevelt.

"Since we are sharing confidences, I also have an awkward history with Ambassador Kennedy," he began, slowly. "Close to a decade ago I entered into some stock investments in firms that were associated with Kennedy. One was a transit company, another a distillery. Brooklyn Manhattan Transit, and the National Distillers Products. It was no secret at the time that I had a mixed history with investments, and I was under growing financial pressures to maintain Chartwell Manor. This was in '34—about the time that Kennedy was very skillfully involving himself in selling British whiskey in the U.S. I sold that stock shortly after---my brother Jack handled the transaction from his brokerage company---and made a decent profit."

"I made a larger investment in the transit stock," Churchill admitted. "I bought shares in several bunches. Kennedy's associate, Barnard Baruch, handled the sale. I remember it was around the time that Kennedy came for a short visit at Chartwell. Unlike some of my other transactions, this one proved quite fruitful. I was looking for some-low priced solid securities to file away for a few years, with no worry about immediate dividends. I got drubbed in the '29 market crash, and I vowed I would invest smarter this time around. Joe Kennedy and his people were guiding me..."

At this point, Roosevelt felt compelled to tell *his* financial story.

"My Joe Kennedy story is a little different," he said. "My son James' company won the insurance contracts with the National Distillers account for the maritime transports and their cargo of liquor en route from England to America. Jimmy negotiated the contract with Seton Porter, Kennedy's contact at National Distillers, while on a trip to London. Jimmy assured me later he got the contract based solely on merit---not on his family name. Jimmy knew there would be a burgeoning liquor market when Prohibition was lifted. He never invested directly in National Distillers' stock, his interest was purely in the insurance business---and he did well at it. You could say that the deal was riding on Kennedy's coattails, since it was Kennedy that landed the National Distillers business in the first place. Jimmy tells me he never used the Roosevelt name to leverage business, but there are never any pure deals when your business is mixed in equal measure with politics."

Churchill gave out a single, sharp laugh, rocked back in his chair, slapping his broad hand to his knee. "And so, here sit we two political warriors---

the Churchills and the Roosevelts---both bound together in a relationship with a man with whom we both now consider oceans apart—a man whom we both have concluded at this stage is a reckless and unstable presence, capable of clear harm if not sidelined."

"Well, Prime Minister," Roosevelt smiled, "I am glad to see us 'united' in some many respects. And I ask you for this one final favor: please keep our conversation this afternoon in complete confidence. It goes without saying that my relationship with Joe Kennedy and his family is still of abiding interest to me. Let this be another one of our Casablanca secrets."

"We are allied in this resolve!" Churchill agreed, with a bright smile.

Churchill rose, and went to the door to summon their staff, who came and wheeled Roosevelt out of the room, while others gathered up the dishes of boiled ham and fruit salad that remained on the plates.

Post Script:

In an "Official Communique on the Casablanca Conference" issued by President Roosevelt on January 26, 1943, the American people were told that the "President of the United States and the Prime Minister of Great Britain have been in conference near Casablanca since January 14...For ten days the combined staffs have been in constant session, meeting two or three times a day and recording progress at intervals to the President and Prime Minister. The entire field of the war was surveyed theater by theater throughout the world, and all resources were marshaled for a more intense prosecution of the war by sea, land, and air. Nothing like this prolonged discussion between two allies has ever taken place before. Complete agreement was reached between the leaders of the two countries and their respective staffs upon war plans and enterprises to be undertaken during the campaigns of 1943 against Germany, Italy, and Japan with a view to drawing the utmost advantage from the markedly favorable turn of events at the close of 1942."

The Communique noted that Premier Stalin had been fully informed of the military proposals, as had Generalissimo Chiang Kai-shek, who was praised for "China's magnificent and unrelaxing struggle for the common cause."

The Communique from President Roosevelt ended by saying, "The President and Prime Minister and their combined staffs, having completed their plans for the offensive campaigns of 1943, have now separated in order to put them into active and concerted execution."

World War II ended two years and four months after the Casablanca Conference.

After he resigned his Ambassadorship to Britain, Joe Kennedy maintained his distance from the Roosevelt presidency. Kennedy was largely disengaged politically for the rest of the war years, although he did some work for Roosevelt's re-election to his final term in 1944.

Although the elder Kennedy had a long-standing aspiration of running for President, he turned his attention to seeing one of his children reach that goal, beginning first with Joe Kennedy, Jr. a Navy pilot bomber whose plane exploded over the English channel.

The senior Kennedy cultivated a close alliance with Republican Senator Joseph McCarthy, who spearheaded the anti-communist inquests by the Senate in the 1950s. Kennedy was a major financial contributor to the Senator from Wisconsin. Kennedy lobbied Senator McCarthy to hire the Ambassador's son, Robert Kennedy, as a staff member of the Senate Investigations committee. The elder Kennedy also played a key backstage role in the management of John F. Kennedy's Senatorial and later Presidential campaign in 1960.

In 1961, Joe Kennedy suffered a stroke which left him partially paralyzed with very limited speech. He lived to see two of his sons assassinated.

Joseph P. Kennedy died in the Fall of 1969 at the family's Hyannis Port, Massachusetts compound at the age of 81.

STREET SWEEPER

"Five and a half years ago, on the morning of January 17, 1989, an anonymous person phoned the Stockton, California Police Department regarding a death threat against Cleveland Elementary School. The tragic events that unfolded from there are part of the reason we are here today in this school-wide assembly."

Dr. Wilma Bonner, Principal of Woodrow Wilson High School in Washington, D.C., cleared her throat, and surveyed her audience. There were approximately 600 students and teachers in the auditorium. Behind her, the school's motto hung on a banner: "Haec olim meminisse juvabit." Bonner adjusted her podium microphone to the level she wanted. She was wearing a tan skirt, a dark blue blazer over a white shirt with a large open collar, from which flowed the two ends of a large floral scarf.

"A person that the police later called 'a disturbed drifter,' parked his Chevy Van behind the school, and set the vehicle on fire. This 24-year-old man then hid behind a portable building on the school playground, and as the children poured out of the school, he began firing at them with a semi-automatic rifle. He fired 106 rounds from his AK-47 rifle in three minutes, wounding 34 children and a teacher. Five children—most of them Cambodian and Vietnamese immigrants—died in that attack. The gunman then took his own life."

"This is truly a shocking story—but I am not telling it to you merely for its shock value. Out of this horrific incident of school violence we must ask ourselves: 'What can we do to prevent any further tragedies like the one that took place at Cleveland Elementary School?'"

Bonner turned to the panelists onstage seated at a table to her left.

"Just a short drive downtown from here, Congress has been grappling with this very issue," Bonner said. "President Clinton recently signed into law the Violent Crime Control and Law Enforcement Act of 1994. Part of this new law creates a federal assault weapons ban. The Stockton shooting---and others like it—have stoked public concerns about mass killings, and the need to restrict the sale of semiautomatic assault weapons, along with large-capacity ammunition magazines. A recent CNN poll found that 77% of Americans support a ban on the manufacture, sale, and possession of such weapons. But will this new law really end assault weapon violence?"

"To help us understand this challenge—which affects the very core of our academic community here at Woodrow Wilson---we have invited three members of Congress who have recently come from the debate on Capitol Hill: U.S. Senator Frank Lautenberg of New Jersey, U.S. Senator Patrick Leahy of Vermont, and U.S. Senator Larry Craig of Idaho. Let me now ask the Woodrow Wilson student body to give these distinguished Senators a warm Green and White welcome this morning..."

As Bonner stepped back from the microphone to applaud her guests, the auditorium responded with polite applause.

"Senator Lautenberg, may I ask you to be the first to jump into this discussion?" Bonner said, turning to the panelists.

Lautenberg pulled his table top microphone closer and tapped it once with his finger for a sound check.

"First, let me thank Dr. Bonner for having the courage and wisdom to bring this conversation—which I know is uncomfortable to us all—to the attention of this great High School class," Lautenberg said.

"Gun violence is destroying America's brightest hope for the future--our children. Here are just two examples taken from the last month---two stories that tell us what can happen when children get their hands on guns. In High Bridge, New Jersey, a 13-year-old boy shot and killed an 11-year-old friend over a silly, childhood argument. In Chicago, Illinois, an 11-year-old boy shot into a crowd, murdered a girl, and was then killed himself--by a 14-year-old and a 16-year-old. Both tragedies demonstrate what happens when kids can gain easy access to guns in our streets and in our homes."

"At a time when our children should be playing in little league, studying algebra, or going to high school dances," Lautenberg said, "they are engaged in deadly street warfare. Instead of notebooks and pencils, they carry guns and bullets. Instead of dreaming about college, 15-year-old boys dream of streets, of gangs, and of semiautomatic handguns. Instead of planning their sweet 16's, 15-year-old girls sit around and plan their funerals."

"We have been trying to get the guns out of our neighborhoods and out of our schools. But each time we try to do it, regressive forces get in the way. Every day 14 American children--14 kids here in America--are killed by guns. But every day, the National Rifle Association gives more than $14 to politicians, orchestrates more than 14 letters, inspires more than 14 phone calls. Few politicians are willing to stand up to such a powerful special interest. So little gets done."

"It took us years to pass the Brady bill--a bill which has already proven to be effective and would have saved thousands of lives if it had been passed when it was proposed 10 years ago. It took us 6 years to get a ban on selected semiautomatic weapons passed. And even then, the NRA wanted to scuttle the entire crime bill---along with all that money for cops and prisons---if that was the price of keeping semi's in their homes and on our streets."

"Well, let me tell every student and teacher in this room: this time the NRA lost. And we won. President Clinton has signed the crime bill, enacting a ban on 19 different assault weapons and prohibiting gun possession by minors. It's a giant step in the right direction---but we cannot forget that it was almost derailed by the NRA."

"We can celebrate today---but we also have to make a commitment today to keep going. To keep fighting. Because according to the National Education Association, more than 100,000 students pack a gun with their school things every morning."

"We all know that guns do not belong in, or near, America's school yards, and we will continue fighting to keep them away. We must remember that this crime bill is not an end to our fight against guns and crime. It is a beginning. We must continue to fight for reasonable gun control: to stand up to those who put their ideology above the safety of our children."

Dr. Bonner stepped back to the podium, adjusting the microphone arm. "Thank you, Senator Lautenberg for those words...I'd like to ask Senator Leahy now to add his comments. Senator?"

Senator Leahy turned on his microphone and glanced down at his yellow pad of notes.

"Like Senator Lautenberg, I would like to commend Dr. Bonner for offering this important forum for Woodrow Wilson students and faculty..."

"I spent nearly 9 years in law enforcement. I know that it is impossible simply to pass a law to stop crime. I carried a badge and I was a prosecutor. But let me say a few words about the assault weapons provision. I get very frustrated by some of the loose talk that goes on in the Congress about guns. A lot of people stand up and give great speeches about banning guns, and it is obvious when you hear them talk that they never fired a gun in their life and they do not know one end from another."

"I grew up in a State where usually from your early teens you are taking gun safety courses, and certainly most people in my generation owned guns and have owned them from the time they were children. I own many guns, and many weekends when I am home in Vermont I love to target shoot."

"But I also know there are weapons that are designed especially for killing people. Let us talk about something like the Street Sweeper. I am not an advocate of sweeping gun control. We have one of the highest per capita ownership of guns in America in Vermont. We also have the lowest crime rate in the country. So there is not this direct correlation between gun control and crime rates as some would have you believe."

"I happen to think that what would help even more than strict gun control in this country would be some strict family control and maybe going back to basic principles that parents know where their children are, that they teach respect for life, that they teach respect for each other and respect for the rights of each other and instill real values."

"But I also know that all the country is not Vermont. I know that there are people who live in terror in our cities, terror that no matter how well they conduct their lives, how law abiding they are, how honest they are, they face the possibility of being killed maybe for $5, maybe because they wore the wrong color clothes, maybe because they just happen to be in the wrong place at the wrong time, even though minding their own business in doing it."

"I know the real fear that Americans are feeling in this country, where they face weapons on the streets of America--the greatest democracy in the world--where they face weapons that would be terrible and terrifying on the battlefields of the world, weapons like the Street Sweeper. I do not know if any of you have actually seen one of these. I have. It is a horrible weapon if you know what it might do."

"When you make something that looks like the old Thompson submachine gun loaded up with a huge magazine full of 12-gauge rounds, sometimes with rifle slugs, sometimes double ought buckshot and you can virtually tear a wall out of a room with it, when you can wipe out not one victim but a crowd of victims---these are not hunting weapons. These are not sporting weapons. Anybody who is a hunter, anybody who values sporting, would be terrified to see someone walking through the woods carrying a weapon of that type."

"How does somebody feel pulling into a gas station and wondering if someone will come out with a weapon like that or walking down a street and wondering if someone might be carrying that, or coming out of a restaurant and wondering if someone going by in a car will be firing something like that?"

"We are no longer a country of wild frontiers. I am perfectly willing to foreclose to myself the ability to own some weapons that I believe I could own safely, manage carefully, and would never use in crime. I am willing to give that up for the safety of this country."

Leahy stopped, and turned to Bonner. "How are we doing for time? I know people have classes to go to..."

"We are fine, Senator," Bonner said. "Please continue..."

"We have a very limited number of guns that are banned in this new law. You would think by some who speak about it that we are disarming America. That is not so. Every Vermonter who now owns guns will still own guns when this bill passes. Every Vermonter will know there are some weapons they may not buy in the future, but no Vermonter is going to buy those weapons to go hunting. They say they may want them for a collector's item. I say to them, collect something else."

"This is a time when we have to say to the American people: The carnage on our streets has gone far enough. The terror that Americans face has gone far enough. This law will not stop the carnage, this will not stop the terror, but it will at least give some hope to the American people that Congress is willing to stand up and will not bow to any lobby anywhere, from the right or the left, but we will try to do what is right."

At this point, several students in the front stood up and loudly applauded the Senator.

"You must be from Vermont," Senator Leahy joked, waving at the students.

Dr. Bonner then announced the final speaker.

"Thank you, Senator Leahy for your passion...Now we will turn to our third honored guest this morning, please welcome U.S. Senator Larry Craig of Idaho..."

Craig turned on his microphone, and like his colleagues, began by thanking Dr. Bonner for inviting him to speak.

"I am a little younger than my two distinguished friends here." Craig began, "but more importantly, I am from a district that has a much different view of this new gun law than the good people of New Jersey, or Vermont. I have represented the voters of Idaho—at the state or federal level—since 1974. I have also been as member of the National Rifle Association since 1983."

"Last week on the floor of the Senate, one of my colleagues said to me: 'Oh, there's that gun nut from Idaho. I bet he would even support the right of somebody to own a bazooka.' That's foolishness. Artillery pieces, tanks, nuclear devices, and other heavy ordnances—none of them are constitutionally protected. Nobody has ever argued that they ought to be."

"The Second Amendment does not provide that any citizen should own a military-type device---like a grenade, a bomb, a bazooka, or other devices. But we know that under the Constitution the right to bear arms does protect the ordinary small arms---handguns, rifles, shotguns, yes, and even those that we now, under this bill, call assault weapons. They are the semiautos."

"Let me suggest to you that the Second Amendment of our Constitution means that the citizen has the right to own and bear an arm not for sporting purposes, not for hunting purposes---but in the right of self-defense, in the right of the protection of one's self and one's property---as our Founding Fathers so clearly spelled out."

"During debate on this bill, I listened to colleagues talk about the NRA as some evil, sinister group who would like to suggest to society that everybody ought to own a gun and walk the streets and use it freely and uninhibited. Well, the NRA is an old organization---been around over 100 years---who believes in the right of the citizen under the Second Amendment. They are not tightly organized. They are not all-powerful. They are a grassroots organization quite typical of a lot of organizations in this country of citizens who come together under a common and oftentimes single interest. Are they strong? Well, they have over 3 million members now."

"Since President Clinton came to the White House, the NRA has been picking up about 10,000 new members a month. Why? Many of those members do not even own a gun. But they are very fearful that this President and some in Congress want to reach out and rob them of their rights under the Constitution."

"So, they come together in organization and they give of their time and of their resource to try to protect those rights. And they do what every other good interest group does: they pick up their phone and they call their Senator or their Representative, and they say, 'Please, please, do something about House Resolution 3355 because it takes away from me the rights that my Founding Fathers gave me under the Constitution.'"

"The American people are frustrated. Many say, yes: get the guns off the streets; people are being killed by the use of a firearm in a criminal act by an individual. They are frustrated and they are angered, and they should be. But what we also understand here is sometimes we have to stand just a little bit beyond the current or the popular idea and say that there is a bigger and a more important issue here; that is, to protect the rights under the Constitution of the free citizen."

"There are some who would have been willing to accept a ban on guns--I am not among those--but who would have put tough penalties into this crime bill that said that a criminal would be punished if he or she used a gun in the commission of a crime."

"I think the American people are very confused as to why Congress will not stand up and say to the criminal element of this society: you are out; you no longer get to play on the streets. But somehow, we will reach out, and in our fright and in our frustration, we will take away the right of the free Citizen. My guess is that someday in the not-too-distant future, after the American people have seen what is embodied in this crime bill, they are going to say to Congress, 'Oh, no, you don't. This is not what we meant at all. What we meant is for you to get tough on criminals and stay tough on criminals and not to take away our rights or misalign our free citizenship.'"

"We do not have a gun problem in America. We have a law enforcement problem. Tough laws are already on the books to remove criminals from society, but they simply have to be used."

Senator Craig turned off his microphone as Dr. Bonner returned to the podium.

"Thank you, Senator Craig for sharing your thoughts with us today," Bonner said.

"We have time for one or two questions before I ask you to return to your homerooms. We will bring a microphone to you if you have a question you'd like to ask any of our panelists..."

A student near the front aisle immediately threw up her hand and rose to wait for a microphone.

"My name is Tiana Williams," she said. "and I'm a Junior. I'd like to ask Mr. Craig a question...You say you are ok with people carrying around these assault weapons like it was their right. So, what would you say to students at Woodrow Wilson if there was mass shooting right here?"

Senator Craig turned his mic on again. "Thank you, Tiana, for that question. What I am saying is that the laws we need are already on the books. Under the Gun Control Act of 1968, it is a Federal felony punishable by a 5-year prison term and a quarter of a million dollar fine for a convicted felon to be in possession of an assault weapon. That is the law now. The 1968 law says you cannot do it now, criminal. If you own an assault weapon, you go to jail."

"But that man in Stockton, California who killed all those kids---he had no criminal record at all---so I'm not talking about convicted felons." the student responded.

Dr. Bonner pointed to a raised hand in the back of the room. "We only have time for one more question....yes, in the back?"

"Hi, my name is Ethan, and I am a Senior. I don't know if this is a question or a statement---and any of you can answer it----but I just want to know what any of you all are going do if these mass killings continue? I mean, how many more of these school shootings are going happen. How many more little kids need to get shot? I mean, we're talking about this today, in 1994---but what if the killing keeps happening? Are kids going to have to pack guns to school to protect themselves? You can pass all the laws you want---but there's a lot of hardware on the streets right now—and I worry that these shootings are not going to stop. What are you going tell kids twenty years from now if the mass shootings don't stop? When does this end?"

Congressman Craig took off his glasses replied: "Young man, let me tell you this: Forcing gun control laws on decent citizens is comparable to Congress passing a law to eradicate cancer by forcing an elderly healthy person to undergo chemotherapy and radiation. It might cure cancer, but it might also kill most of us in the process."

Dr. Bonner jumped in. "Ethan, that's a great question---one that unfortunately has no short answer! Let me remind everyone that your Period One classes have been cancelled, because we are getting a late start. If you had gym this morning, those classes will be rescheduled later in the week."

"Thank you all for coming this morning, and let's thank all our special guests from Congress, who left us with much to think about..."

Post Script:

In 1994, the Violent Crime Control and Law Enforcement Act (Public Law 103-322) provided funding for 100,000 new police officers, nearly $10 billion for prisons and $6.1 billion for crime prevention programs. The law included a Federal Assault Weapons Ban, which barred the manufacture of

19 specific kinds of semi-automatic firearms, including magazines holding more than ten rounds of ammunition. The Act made possession of firearms by certain people a federal death penalty offense. The law took effect September 13, 1994 but it ended ten years later due to a "sunset" provision placed in the bill. As a result, magazines carrying more than ten rounds of ammunition were legal again.

The law also created dozens of new death penalty offenses, including acts of terrorism and civil-rights related murders. The law earmarked $1.6 billion to prevent violence against women, which was extended beyond the ten-year life of the original bill. The law established mechanisms for states to track sex offenders and added $30 billion for the hiring of community police officers at the state and local level. The crime bill made membership in gangs a crime.

Patrick Leahy is still serving in the U.S. Senate, where he has represented Vermont since 1975.

Senator Frank Lautenberg was a 5 term U.S. Senator representing New Jersey. In 2013 he died in Manhattan from viral pneumonia while still serving in the Senate. He was 89.

In 1999, Senator Larry Craig criticized President Bill Clinton over the Monica Lewinsky sex scandal. "The American people already know that Bill Clinton is a bad boy--a naughty boy." Eight years later, Senator Larry Craig pleaded guilty to a misdemeanor disorderly conduct charge stemming from his arrest at the Minneapolis-St. Paul International Airport. Craig was arrested by a plainclothes police officer investigating complaints of lewd behavior in an airport men's room. Senator Craig denied any inappropriate conduct and said later, "I was not involved in any inappropriate conduct... I should not have pled guilty. I was trying to handle this matter myself quickly and expeditiously." Craig insisted, "I am not gay. I never have been gay."

In 2014, a federal judge ordered Senator Craig to pay the U.S. Treasury $242,000 for improperly using campaign funds to pay for his legal defense from his sex-sting arrest in Minnesota.

Craig served 10 years in the U.S. House and 18 years in the U.S. Senate. At a news conference in 2007, Craig announced his intent to resign, but decided later that despite his previous decision, he would serve out his

Senate term. Craig did not seek reelection in 2008 and left office on January 3, 2009.

The provisions in the Violent Crime Control and Law Enforcement Act of 1994 which prohibited the manufacture, transfer, or possession of "semiautomatic assault weapons," as defined by the Act, expired on September 13, 2004.

PEACE THROUGH CORN

For the longest time, Soviet Premier Nikita Khrushchev had been "curious" about the United States---but nobody invited him to come.

He told his son-in-law, Alexei Adzhubei. of his desire to visit Disneyland, and Adzhubei mentioned it to Soviet Ambassador to the United States Mikhail Menshikov, who passed the request on to U.S. Undersecretary of State Robert Murphy.

Khrushchev had another motivation. He wanted his legacy to include being the first Premier of Russia to "open up" America. "The closest Joseph Stalin ever came to America was in 1945 in the Vorontsov Palace at Yalta," Khrushchev joked to Adzhubei. "He was sitting with his hands folded to the left of Franklin D. Roosevelt." "We will make a little American history," Adzhubei later recalled Khruschev saying.

Undersecretary Murphy mentioned the Khrushchev visit idea to Henry Cabot Lodge, the American Ambassador to the United Nations, and Lodge brought plans for a 12 day visit in 1959 from the Premier to President Dwight Eisenhower in the White House. Lodge told the President he was "willing to serve as 'Sergeyevich's' tour guide." Eisenhower confided with Lodge that the Soviet visit raised some security concerns, and Khrushchev's unpredictable demeanor made him a "loose Russian cannon." But the President reluctantly agreed that a Soviet visit might result in a thaw in the Cold War between the two nations.

The final itinerary for the Premier's tour took him to five stops after the nation's capital—to New York, California, Iowa, Pennsylvania, and ending at Camp David. A plan to visit Disneyland was vetoed for security reasons, which prompted Khrushchev to send a pointed note to Lodge saying he was "most displeased" with the cancellation. At dinner one evening, Khrushchev brought up the sore issue of Disneyland: "Do you have rocket launching pads there?" he asked. "What is it? Is there an epidemic of cholera or plague there? Or have gangsters taken hold of the place that can destroy me? And I say I would very much like to go and see Disneyland. For me such a situation is inconceivable."

One stop that remained on the official itinerary was to a wide spot in the road called Coon Rapids, Iowa. On September 22nd, Khrushchev flew to Des Moines, Iowa, where he visited a meat-packing plant, and tasted his first American hot dog, telling reporters, "We have beaten you to the moon, but you have beaten us in sausage making."

The following morning, the Premier and his entourage drove 70 miles to Coon Rapids to the farm of Roswell "Bob" Garst. Khrushchev had met Garst four years earlier when the Iowan had visited Russia to give lectures on the use of hybrid seed corn and fertilizers to boost crop yield.

At the time, Khrushchev was drawn to the Iowa farmer. He told friends that Garst was "a very interesting conversationalist who knew agriculture well…He sold Russians thousands of tons of his corn. He is a good model for capitalists."

Khrushchev had an understandable affinity for the entrepreneurial Iowan farmer. As a child growing up in Kalinovka at the end of the 19th century, Khrushchev took a job taking care of cattle, which continued until he was in his early teens. "You know," Garst told Khrushchev, as the two were walking around the Coon Rapids fields, "we two farmers could settle the problems of the world faster than diplomats."

Garst pitched the Premier about a theory he called "Peace Through Corn." Garst wanted to convince Khrushchev that if his country would produce better crops, it could foster world peace. "It would be dangerous," Garst argued, "for the world to have a Russia that is both hungry and has the H-bomb. I never saw a well-fed, contented man who was really dangerous." Under Garst's plan, Americans would raise corn, the Soviets would buy it, and they would all live together in peace.

This was really not a hard sell to Khrushchev. He wanted to see Russia planting more corn. He helped establish a corn institute in the Ukraine, sponsored a Corn Pavilion in Moscow, and earmarked vast acres of land in Kazakhstan for corn production. Khrushchev was fascinated with Garst's mechanized feed system in his cattle barns, and the steel pipes and sprinkler system he used to irrigating his fields—methods not well known in the Soviet Union. In 1955 Khrushchev send a delegation to Garst's farm to

117

study Garst's farming techniques, and Garst was invited to visit Russia, which is when he spent time in Khrushchev's dacha on the Black Sea.

One afternoon, when the two were swimming together, Khrushchev asked Garst if he would ever consider moving to Moscow? "We have enormous amount of land for corn," the Premier said. "You could be our Premier of Corn."

Garst, himself a large man like Khrushchev, told the Premier: "I'm just a little dirt farmer from Iowa, Nikita. I don't think I could put up with your winters in Moscow."

Four years later, as the two friends were walking along the long rows of shoulder-high corn stalks, Khruschev turned to Garst, and lowered his voice as he spoke: "Tell me something: why do you think your government does not want me to see Disneyland? Maybe weapons? I think you have weapons there, yes? I was very disappointed to miss Disneyland."

"Look, Nikita," Garst replied, "I know a lot about corn. You can ask me anything you want about corn. But I know nothing about weapons."

Khrushchev grew silent. He lifted his head, and his eyes moved over the lush green countryside in front of him.

"You know, Bob," he continued, putting an arm on Garst's shoulder, "my predecessor Mr. Stalin, would never be here talking like this to you. He did not ever want to come here. But I have traveled a long way to see you again, my friend. I think if there are weapons at Disneyland, you should be honest with me. I have been totally honest with you."

"You are a farmer, you are not like Mr. Lodge, or those other representatives in your government. I know your President did not want me to visit Disneyland—and it was not because he did not want me to meet that little mouse with the white gloves and the button pants. No, my friend, there is more going on here than amusement parks..."

"I'm sorry, Premier," Garst stumbled, unsure of where to go next with this conversation, "but I have not been told a thing about weapons, and they told me we were going to talk about raising corn."

At that moment, Garst spied a swarm of photographers tramping across his cornfield heading towards him and the Premier. Waving both arms above his head, Garst yelled, "You fellows get out of the way. I'm gonna kick you out of the way if you don't turn around!" Garst bent down and scooped out a handful of wet silage, and threw it at the photographers, who rapidly snapped photos of Garst blocking their path to the Premier. Garst even wildly kicked at one reporter from the *New York Times*. "Locusts!" he yelled at them, as they scattered in retreat.

When Garst turned back to Khrushchev, the Premier was shaking with laughter. He grabbed Garst's right arm by the wrist and said to him: "Bob, promise me now that you will not mention our Disneyland discussion today. Forget our discussion about the Mouse. I will get to Disneyland someday---but it will be on my own terms. Do you understand?"

"Yeah, sure, Garst stammered.

On their way back to the farmhouse, several farmhands were making their way across the field. They were large-limbed women. The Premier pulled Garst close to him, gripping him again tightly by one wrist. "You know," he said, with a little smile, "the Persians believed that a large belly and rump were signs of prosperity and good fortune. These people who work your land---they are eating well. I think these women are good advertisements for capitalism. I wish that we Russians all looked like that."

Slowly turning a shiny yellow corn cob in his hands, the Premium pivoted squarely to Garst. "Or, maybe, someday, you will all look like us." he laughed.

As Khrushchev turned to walk towards the farm house in the distance, he looked back one last time at Garst. "And you tell that little Mouse: I will be back next time to see his missiles for sure!"

Post Script:

Roswell Garst's 53-acre farm in Guthrie County, Iowa was designated a National Historic Preservation Trust site in 2009—50 years after the visit of Premier Khrushchev. After the Premier's visit, the U.S. government said that the Iowa stop was one of the most significant parts of Khrushchev's tour, because it inspired the Premier to return to Russia with new ideas for reforming Russian agricultural practices. Garst wrote a book entitled Letters from an American Farmer: The Eastern European and Russian Correspondence of Roswell Garst. *Garst died in 1977 at the age of 79.*

Although Nikita Khrushchev was unable to visit Disneyland while he was in Los Angeles, he was able to visit the studios of Twentieth Century Fox to watch the filming of the Broadway musical Can-Can. The studio held a luncheon for the Premier in its swanky commissary. A cluster of Hollywood stars showed up: including Elizabeth Taylor, Bob Hope, Marilyn Monroe, Judy Garland, Gary Cooper, Henry Fonda, Kirk Douglas, Jack Benny, and Frank Sinatra.

Khrushchev was seated at the head table. His wife, Nina, told Bob Hope that she wanted to see Disneyland. Los Angeles Police Chief William Parker initially assured Henry Cabot Lodge that he could provide security for any such visit, but later he refused to accept responsibility for Khrushchev's safety if he went to the Disney theme park—and the meeting was crossed off the agenda. Khrushchev sent a note to Lodge that he was "most displeased" by the cancellation.

Khrushchev told the media, "Just now, I was told that I could not go to Disneyland. I asked, 'Why not? What is it? Is there an epidemic of cholera there? Have gangsters taken hold of the place? Your policemen are so tough they can lift a bull by the horns. Surely, they can restore order if there are any gangsters around. I say, 'I would very much like to see Disneyland.' They say, 'We cannot guarantee your security.' Then what must I do, commit suicide?"

After Khrushchev returned to Russia, he remained in power for another five years until the Fall of 1964, when he was ousted by opponents. Khrushchev agreed to voluntarily leave office due to "advanced age and ill health." Khrushchev spent four years writing his memoirs Khrushchev Remembers. *His writings were denounced in the Russian press, and the manuscript had to be smuggled out of the Soviet Union and published in the West.*

Khrushchev lived seven years in a form of internal exile in Russia and died of a heart attack in a hospital near his home in Moscow in the Fall of 1971, at the age of 77. Neither he, nor his wife Nina, ever visited Disneyland.

GET WORD TO HOOVER

Secretary of State George Marshall stood on the podium at Harvard University on a warm afternoon in June of 1947, having just received an honorary degree from University President James Conant. Looking out across the crowd of roughly 15,000 people who had assembled in Harvard Yard, he told the crowd he was "profoundly grateful and touched by the great distinction and honor that you have bestowed upon me, and I am overwhelmed, as a matter of fact, and rather fearful of my inability to maintain such a high rating as you've been generous enough to bestow on me."

Marshall told university officials that he did not plan to give a major speech to the Harvard Alumni Association. He had not circulated the speech to anyone outside of the State Department. The media had not been alerted. In fact, to draw attention away from the speech, President Truman called a press conference in Washington, D.C for the same time. The Truman Administration had decided that Marshall's remarks should be low-keyed for its American audience---but played up in Europe. He wanted to build up support in Europe before promoting the plan in the States.

Dean Acheson, an Under Secretary of State, was assigned to distribute Marshall's speech widely to the British and European media. Acheson was able to get the speech read in its entirely on the BBC.

The speech that afternoon was not called "The Marshall Plan." It was still thought of as "The European Recovery Program," and its purpose was to funnel $13 billion to help underwrite the economic recovery of Europe between 1948 and 1951. The intent was to trigger economic restoration in Europe, and instill confidence among the European people themselves in their post-war economic future. But the plan would also open up new markets and demand for U.S. goods. The United States would shape the European economy to better support the American economy.

In the throng at Harvard Yard listening were two men who had come separately, but who spotted one another in the crowd. They both knew the importance of what Marshall was about to present.

One of the men near the podium was Charles "Chip" Bohlen, who had served in Russia during World War II, was considered an expert on the Soviet Union, and was fluent in Russian. He had served at the Department of State for nearly 20 years and had traveled on missions to Joseph Stalin in Moscow.

Bohlen was FDR's interpreter at the Yalta Conference in 1945. When General George Marshall became Secretary of State in 1947, Bohlen was positioned as a key adviser to President Harry Truman. It was Chip Bohlen who had written the first draft of the speech Marshall was about to deliver. Working with State Department memos, Bolen had repeated descriptions of post-War Europe as teetering on the edge of destruction. "Millions of people in the cities are slowly starving," he had written, and if something were not done soon to lift the standard of living, "there will be revolution."

Standing next to Bolen was Frank Wisner, who had served as the head of the Office of Strategic Services (OSS) operations in Southern Europe at the end of World War II. A Wall Street lawyer who joined the Navy at the outbreak of the war, Wisner had seen a train full of Germans being sent to a labor camp in Russia, and he never forgave the Soviet Union. After the War, Wisner was recruited to join the State Department's Office of Occupied Territories, then was promoted to 1st Director of the new 'Special Projects' unit.

In 1948, he became Executive Director of the renamed Office of Policy Coordination (OPC), which worked with the CIA. Under OPC's secret charter, Wisner was put in charge of propaganda, economic warfare, preventive direct action, including sabotage, antisabotage, demolition and evacuation procedures; subversion against hostile states, including assistance to underground resistance groups, guerrillas and refugee liberation groups, support of indigenous anti-communist elements in threatened free world countries, and creation of "stay-behind" networks all over Europe after U.S. withdrawal. He was a veteran under-cover operative.

The two men looked around the crowd as Marshall spoke, to see if there were others in attendance they should recognize---or avoid.

"How is Polly?" Bohlen asked Wisner. "How are Elizabeth and Ellis? Anything new with Graham or little Frank?"

"Polly is great, thanks. Not much change elsewhere." Wisner replied. "I am hoping that Frank will eventually find his way into the diplomatic service." And how's your family?"

"Pretty much the same," Bohlen said. As Marshall began his speech, both men pivoted back to face the podium.

"I need not tell you that the world situation is very serious." Marshall began, leaning into the podium. "That must be apparent to all intelligent people. I think one difficulty is that the problem is one of such enormous complexity that the very mass of facts presented to the public by press and radio make it exceedingly difficult for the man in the street to reach a clear appraisement of the situation..."

"Chip, did you write this?" Wisner asked.

"I had a hand in it," Bohlen nodded, "The Secretary himself did the final cut. When he met with Stalin, the idea for a major economic plan was born. The Secretary felt that Stalin wanted to delay negotiations until Western Europe collapsed. The Secretary told me that Stalin was 'waiting for Europe to fall in his lap.'"

"You can't trust the Generalissmo---or Molotov," Wisner added. "They play by their own communist rules."

"We don't trust anyone at this point. The Secretary gave me orders that no one was to publicize this speech. You don't see a lot of press here today. If there was lots of publicity, we were afraid that members of congress would get into the act. We need European action first. Then we can come back and sell it in the U.S."

"The key to the future of Europe is not what we say we're going to do," Wisner said, "but the covert action we take that no one knows we're doing."

Bohlen scowled at this thought. "I think the genius of this plan is that we saw the need for America to help jump-start Europe's engine. Let's toss the ball to Europe and let them do what they can."

"I've been briefed on the CIA funds in your plan," Wisner said—unsure if Bohlen knew these details. "About 5% of these funds are earmarked for secret ops abroad. My OPC will direct that funding. We're talking about creating false front organizations to manipulate the affairs of foreign countries. Propaganda campaigns against sitting governments. Illegal underground opposition groups, infiltrating labor unions...This is how change happens..."

Wisner stopped to gauge Bohler's reaction. Seeing none, he continued.

"You remember the Nightingale battalion? Guerilla group in the Ukraine? We're going to create a common front with other Ukrainian nationalists and the Ukrainian Insurgent Army. We're going to crack Russia's control over the Ukraine!"

Bohlen stopped him. "Whoa. That Nightingale group are the folks who murdered thousands of Russians, Poles and Jews during the war. This is not what the Marshall Plan is all about..."

"Any assistance that this Government may render in the future," Marshall continued into the microphone, "should provide a cure rather than a mere palliative."

Marshall's voice was echoing slightly off the brick university walls.

"Any government which maneuvers to block the recovery of other countries cannot expect help from us. Furthermore, governments, political parties or groups which seek to perpetuate human misery in order to profit therefrom politically, or otherwise, will encounter the opposition of the United States."

Wisner stepped closer to Bohlen and dropped his voice almost to a whisper. "Did you know that Hoover's been using the FBI to monitor some of my boys?" Wisner asked. "He described them as 'Wisner's gang of weirdos.' I'm hearing that he thinks some of my guys have been active in left-wing politics more than a decade ago. This is not helpful, Chip. I mean, if you want to talk about weirdos, J. Edgar belongs at the top of the list."

"Two years after the close of hostilities," Marshall was telling the audience, "a peace settlement with Germany and Austria has not been agreed upon...the rehabilitation of the economic structure of Europe quite evidently will require a much longer time and greater effort than had been foreseen."

"Hoover's been snooping around my relationship with that Romanian Princess—you know---Princess Caradja? He thinks she's a Soviet spy," Wisner said, wiping his mouth with a handkerchief. "During the war, Caradja helped thousands of downed Allied flyers escape from Romania into Italy. They called her the 'Angel of Ploiești.' She's a goddamn war hero, Chip, not an agent for Chrissakes."

"I was working in Bucharest at the time as the head of OSS operations. That's how I meet the Princess." Wisner said. "We spent some time together. I was a long way from home and working under a lot of pressure. We were very discreet. But someone got it into Hoover's head that Caradja was a spy for the Soviets. He passed that intelligence onto Senator McCarthy, who's been surveilling me!"

"Who is *Hoover* to be investigating people's alleged sexual activity?" Wisner asked. "He's got his own problems in that department. Where does he get the right to monitor my comings and goings?"

"Watch yourself, Frank." Bohlen warned. "Don't underestimate Hoover's reach."

"It is logical," Marshall continued, turning a page of his speech, "that the United States should do whatever it is able to do to assist in the return of normal economic health in the world, without which there can be no political stability and no assured peace. Our policy is directed not against any country or doctrine but against hunger, poverty, desperation and chaos."

"Can you get Hoover off my back?" Wisner pleaded. "I need to get him onto another scent. He may have me wiretapped for all I know. Doesn't he have enough commies to chase? If McCarthy calls me to testify before Congress things could get really ugly fast."

"That's crazy talk," Bohlen said. "Hoover would never tap you."

"Oh, yeah? Well, it's got Polly upset—I can tell you that. If she ever gets wind of this Caradja thing--I've got a lot of damage to repair…"

"Governments, political parties or groups which seek to perpetuate human misery in order to profit therefrom politically or otherwise," Marshall warned the crowd, "will encounter the opposition of the United States. Europe's requirements for the next three or four years of foreign food and other essential products-principally from America-are so much greater than her present ability to pay that she must have substantial additional help, or face economic, social and political deterioration of a very grave character."

"I've been married for 18 years, Chip." Wisner said flatly. "Things like this could wreck *every*thing. If Hoover ever breathes a word of this publicly, I will not be responsible for my actions."

Bohlen looked down at his shoes.

"Chip, do you know anyone over there that could put in a word with Hoover's people? I'm really at my wit's end..."

Chip turned an ear toward the dais. "Frank, listen to this part of the speech—we edited this part several times..."

"An essential part of any successful action on the part of the United States," Marshall said, lowering his fist to the podium, "is an understanding on the part of the people of America of the character of the problem and the remedies to be applied. Political passion and prejudice should have no part. With foresight, and a willingness on the part of our people to face up to the vast responsibility which history has clearly placed upon our country, the difficulties I have outlined can, and will, be overcome."

A wave of applause from the crowd worked its way from the rear of Harvard yard front to the stage.

At the conclusion of Marshall's speech, Wisner considered standing in a queue waiting to see the Secretary, but after moving up slowly in the line, decided better of it.

Chip Bolen was gathering up his things to leave, when Wisner walked by him on his way out of the Yard.

"Chip," Wisner said, offering his hand, "If you can get word to Hoover, Polly and I would really appreciate it."

"I'll see what I can do. No promises." Bohlen said, shaking Wisner's hand as they parted.

"No promises," Wisner repeated as he turned to look for the gate out. "As I told you: We don't trust anyone at this point."

Post Script:

The so-called European Recovery Program, better known as the "Marshall Plan," was signed President Harry Truman in the Spring of 1948. The Plan authorized $5 billion in aid to 16 European countries. Over the four years in which the plan was implemented, the United States donated $17 billion in economic and technical assistance to help European nations recover from World War II. The less obvious goal of the Marshall Plan was to marginalize the efforts of the Communist movements inside these nations.

To counter American spending, the Russians offered their own economic plan, known as the Molotov Plan. By 1952, as Marshall Plan funding wound down, the economy of the European nations had grown above their post-war economy by 35% higher on average than their pre-war economy. The European Recovery Plan played some role in that prosperity, but a period of recovery after the war likely would have occurred even in the absence of this financial stimulus.

Just as significant, The Marshall Plan helped in the integration of post-war Europe, encouraging trade between nations and creating a framework of economic development of the entire continent.

In 1951 the Marshall Plan was phased out by a Mutual Security Plan, which continued to provide funds to Europe.

Chip Bohlen was appointed by President Eisenhower as Ambassador to Russia in1953. But Bohlen had a falling out with the Eisenhower Administration, and after four years as Ambassador was pressured to resign.

Bohlen served for two years as ambassador to the Philippines, followed by six years as Ambassador to France under Presidents Kennedy and Johnson. Bohlen left government service in 1969, and died at home in Washington, D.C.in 1974 at the age of 69. In 2006, the United States Postal Service issued a Charles Bohlen postage stamp.

In 1947 Frank Wisner went to work for the State Department's Office of Occupied Territories. A year later he was redeployed to a new Office of Special Projects unit, still working for the State Department. Wisner became the first Director of Special Projects, which changed its name in 1948 to the Office of Policy Coordination. As Assistant Director for the OPC,

Wisner's responsibilities included propaganda, economic warfare, sabotage, and subversion against hostile states. His work involved supporting indigenous anti-communist groups in foreign nations.

FBI Director J. Edgar Hoover maintained surveillance over Wisner and suggested that he and some of his operatives had been involved in Communist politics in the 1930s. Hoover shared his Wisner files with U.S. Senator Joe McCarthy, who was building a dossier on staff of the OPC. The FBI monitored details of Wisner's trysts with Romanian Princess Caradja, who the FBI labeled as a Russian spy.

Despite this, Wisner was appointed the second Deputy Director of Plans, a clandestine government group that had access to Central Intelligence Agency staff and funding. Wisner worked secretly to overthrow a regime in Iran and Guatemala.

Hoover and Senator McCarthy continued to monitor Wisner and his staff, and in 1953 succeeded in getting one of Wisner's key staff members fired against Wisner's wishes. Wisner also worked on the U-2 spy plane program that proved to be an embarrassment to the American government when one of these spy planes was shot down over the Soviet Union by a surface to air missile.

In 1958, Wisner was suffering from severe depression and spent six months in a psychiatric hospital in Maryland. Wisner was appointed the Chief of the CIA's London office in 1959, and two years later he was assigned to oversee CIA activities in the distant outpost of British Guiana. After serving in that British Colony for one year, Wisner quit the CIA.

Roughly three years later, in the Fall of 1965, Wisner committed suicide. He was 56 years old.

LANDSLIDE IN NOVEMBER

On the afternoon of July 17,1964, White House speechwriter Horace Busby, Jr. received a call from President Lyndon Johnson's office asking him to meet the President at 8:00 am the following morning in the Treaty Room, to debrief on the acceptance speeches given the night before at the Republican National Convention at the Cow Palace in San Francisco by Senator Barry Goldwater and his running mate, Representative William Miller of New York. LBJ admitted that he had watched almost every minute of the Republican convention, the way a predatory animal watches to learn how its prey's body moves.

Busby was often called on short notice by the President, especially on trips abroad, including sessions at which Johnson would summon him at bedtime, asking Busby to stay with him until he was asleep. Johnson called it "gentling down" with him, as one would do with a race horse. When he thought the President has slipped off to sleep, Busby would quietly go to leave, but as he was easing his way out, Johnson would often call out: "Buzz, are you still there?"

This morning was quite different. When Busby entered the Treaty Room, with its dark green walls and early Victorian pattern carpet, and the prominent Grant-era chandelier hanging from the center of the room, he saw Johnson already seated, long legs crossed, with a Texas-sized cup of coffee, and a copy of the *New York Times* spread out on a desk that just nine months earlier had been the used by the late President Kennedy to sign the Partial Nuclear Test Ban Treaty.

"Buzz!" said the President, taking off his glasses, as his aide entered. "I hope you're feeling as good about the convention show last night as I am!"

Johnson was beaming, hair neatly combed back, dark suit, white shirt and red tie, looking eager and confident to dive into the Republicans' performance. The President had a reputation as an avid campaigner, and last night, the opening bell of the Presidential race had gone off.

Busby jumped right in, as a White House staffer brought him a cup of coffee to a side table. "I thought Miller's speech was a snooze! He said absolutely nothing."

"Yes," Johnson added. "It was flat as the High Plains. Did you see that Congressman Miller called Goldwater the 'Senator from Indiana?' He spent more time praising Eisenhower on his farm in Gettysburg, than the idea of Goldwater in the White House."

"It was a great convention for us," Busby agreed. "Seventy percent of the delegates--acting on Goldwater's instructions--voted down a platform plank affirming the constitutionality of the Civil Rights Act. They just lost the South—and the North---on that one."

"I love this description of Goldwater from *The New York Times*: 'Senator Goldwater is mild-mannered, bespectacled, speaking usually in a quiet voice, and with almost no gestures...He offered no quarter to the moderate Republicans.'"

The President turned back a couple of pages of the newspaper and slid it across the table to Busby. "And we managed to get a three-column story on page One of *The Times* about the economy: "Notable advances have been made in the national economy, gains for the rest of the year would be even greater. Personal income, in particular, has grown faster than the Administration expected, Mr. Johnson said, consumer spending is up, people are in a better position to buy more in the months ahead. Jobs are up 1.4 million since June of last year.'"

Busby turned the paper to page 6 and pushed it back over to Johnson: "There was another three-column piece about the President and Lady Bird taking a 'brisk stroll' through Lafayette Square. It was actually a pretty good news day for us---considering it's the day after the Republican's headline event."

"I should take a walk around the White House more often," Johnson laughed.

"The reporters weren't too kind to Representative Miller," Busby read: 'He has become known for his caustic tongue and a dedication to conservatism. Miller called Truman a 'hatchet man,' and accused John Kennedy of putting on a 'smoothly rehearsed crybaby performance.' Miller was described as 'somewhat cocky in bearing, dressing with a certain elegance...wears a pearl gray homburg.'"

"The Congressman has a rating of 11% from Americans for Democratic Action," the President added. "I don't think he could even take Upstate, New York. Glad we got Miller instead of Scranton. That was a break."

"Miller took a jab at you when he said 'there are only two businesses better off today than they were under the Republican Party: the seat belt industry in Texas, and the paint business in Washington to white wash investigations.' Nobody remembers that story about your driving, and nobody understands the reference to that Robert Baker business in the Senate.'"

"Organized labor hates Miller from the Bell Aircraft strike in '49," Johnson recalled. "The Negroes remember that Miller voted against the civil rights bill in 1956."

"Miller's coverage wasn't a total loss," Busby said. "*The Times* says his wife is 'regarded as a standout in the current crop of good-looking political wives.'

Johnson smiled and said, "Good thing that quote didn't come from me. The League of Women Voters would not be pleased."

"I did learn that Miller plays a good game of billiards, golfs in the low 80s, and smokes around a pack of cigarettes a day. He likes to drink scotch and water," Busby said. "And he was planning to retire from politics this year."

The President leaned back in his chair. "I believe we will help Congressman Miller retire in November. He'll have a lot of time to play billiards after the votes are counted."

"Goldwater is telling the press that he chose Miller 'because he drives Johnson nuts.'" Busby smirked. "He also pledged to wage a 'vigorous campaign' that 'will not be a personal attack. It will be a campaign waged on the issues solely. I've never believed that anybody enhances their position or their beliefs by delving into rumors and gossip about the opponents. I know President Johnson very well. I know the conduct of his campaign will be like mine.'"

Johnson replied: "Damned right it will! Buzz---any goddam rumors or gossip we can dig up on Mr. Goldwater or Mr. Miller is fair game. I predict that their campaign will go negative even before our convention in August."

Busby read from another story: "A reporter asked Goldwater: 'There have been Negro demonstrations out there (outside the Cow Palace). Do you think this is a foretaste of troubles for your campaign?'" And Goldwater answered: "Not if they keep it at a decent level...but if it becomes necessary to have arrests made, then I think they're hurting their own cause. They didn't present a very pretty picture to America tonight, to see this happening."

"Goldwater forgets that he's on record calling you 'the biggest faker in the United States.'" Busby noted.

Johnson, pulling on his ear, smiled: "That's what I would expect from the biggest liar in the United States."

Busby continued to read: "When Goldwater was asked if this was going to be a hard-hitting campaign, the candidate replied: 'Oh, I think you're going to find some brickbats flying around all over the place, but I have nothing personal against him.'"

"I like this quote from Barry," Busby said, lifting up the newspaper: "'I wouldn't be in this thing if I thought I was going to lose. I'm too old to go back to work, and too young to get out of politics. A Democrat has never beaten me—and I don't intend to start letting him at this late date.'"

"A Democrat has never beaten Goldwater because he's never run for any public office outside of Arizona," Johnson smiled. "But he's running in a national marathon this time."

"Did you see Martin Luther King's comment today?" Busby asked: 'I don't consider Mr. Goldwater to be a racist, the Senator articulates a philosophy which gives aid and comfort to the racists.'"

"I like that!" Johnson said, slapping his right hand on the table. 'Aid and comfort to the racists.' That's a whole lot better coming from Dr. King than from me."

"And Whitney Young from the Urban League said Goldwater was appealing 'to all of the fearful, the insecure, prejudiced people in our society," Busby said. 'It's a test of all Americans: whether they believe in democracy, in sharing, in civil rights for all people.'"

Busby took another sip of coffee, and then pointed to an article further back in the paper. "James Farmer at CORE predicted 'a landslide for President Johnson.' He said Goldwater 'has no program. He is just against everything.' CORE had 300 protestors outside the Cow Palace singing 'We Shall Overcome.' And Roy Wilkinson at the NAACP said: 'Goldwater himself is not regarded as a racist, but his supporters are some of the most outspoken racists in America. The federal government must act to protect the rights of citizens against infringement by the state. The Senator believes that Government has no such role."

The President held up one hand and began ticking off his points with his other index finger: "Goldwater stands for less regulation of business; more regulation of labor; less spending for housing and urban renewal; less government spending altogether; local control over education; and an unregulated farm economy."

Busby stood for a moment to return his coffee for a fill up.

"Mr. President," he said, "we've got only a few weeks to assemble your acceptance speech for Atlantic City. What did you think of the Senator's acceptance speech last night? I heard a few memorable lines—not many. And I heard a lot of high-sounding talk that I think, quite frankly, went right over the heads of the American people."

Busby, read from his underlined copy of a transcript of Goldwater's speech: 'The good Lord raised this mighty Republic to be a home for the brave and to flourish as the land of the free not to stagnate in the swampland of collectivism not to cringe before the bullying of communism.'

"He made a couple of nasty references to Vietnam," Busby said: 'Failures mark the slow death of freedom in Laos. Failures infest the jungles of Vietnam.' And then he added: 'We are at war in Vietnam...yet the President, who is the commander-in-chief of our forces, refuses to say whether or not the objective over there is victory.... tragically letting our finest men die on battlefields unmarked by purpose, unmarked by pride, or the prospect of victory.'"

"I expect to hear that crap until election day," Johnson replied. "He's got no battle plan for Vietnam. He's got no briefing book for Laos—just a bunch of stones to throw at the White House."

"'We are tonight a world divided,' Busby continued reading from the Goldwater transcript. 'We are a nation becalmed. We have lost the brisk pace of diversity and the genius of individual creativity. We are plodding along at a pace set by centralized planning red tape...Rather than useful jobs in our country, our people have been offered bureaucratic make-work. rather than moral leadership. They have been given bread and circuses. They have been given spectacles, and yes, they've even been given scandals.'"

"What in hell is he talking about?" Johnson interrupted. "'Bread and Circuses? Scandals?'" My ass. Is he calling VISTA and the Peace Corps 'make-work'? He even criticized NASA's moon program.'"

"Did you get his reference to the street demonstrations at the Cow Palace last night? 'Tonight there is violence in our streets, corruption in our highest offices, aimlessness amongst our youth, and anxiety among our elders....'"

"Goldwater's going to hit hard on public safety," Busby said. "He's trying to scare the shit out of voters: 'Security from domestic violence, no less than from foreign aggression, is the most elementary and fundamental purpose of any government---and a government that cannot fulfill this perfect purpose is one that cannot long command the loyalty of its citizens---nothing prepares the way for tyranny more than the failure of public officials to keep the streets safe from bullies and marauders.'"

"What's this 'hellish tyranny' that he's talking about?" the President scoffed. "All this fear-mongering about 'personal safety to life, to limb, and property in homes, in churches, on the playgrounds.' What's *his* plan? Water cannons in the streets?"

"He's playing to the evangelicals," Busby noted. 'A world in which earthly power can be substituted for divine will...this nation was founded upon the rejection of that notion and upon the acceptance of God as the author of freedom.'

"Am I running against Billy Graham, for Chrissake?" Johnson sputtered. "That speech last night had the ring of a tent sermon."

"That was the intention," Busby said. "He's calling you a dictator: 'Absolute power does corrupt, and those who seek it must be suspect and must be opposed...it leads first to conformity and then to despotism.'"

"I think the American people know there's not a lick of difference between Goldwater and Toilet water," Johnson said, with a deadpan expression.

"His final comments about our great American future sounded like America First to me," Busby said: 'I seek an America proud of its past, proud of its ways, proud of its dream, and determined actively to proclaim them. But our example to the world must, like charity, begin at home.'

"Mr. President, did you see what happened when Goldwater made his 'extremism in the defense of Liberty' quote near the end? Senator Keating and a large group of New York delegates got up and walked right out of the Convention hall. And Congressman John Lindsay told the media he would have to do some 'soul searching' about whether to drop out of the Republican party."

"You can see the fault lines in the Republican Party cracking," Johnson said. "This is the script we wanted."

Johnson stood up and walked out of the room. "Have to take a piss. Be right back. I got something to show you."

When Johnson returned to the Treaty Room, he was carrying some papers with him. He sat down again and pulled his chair closer to Busby.

"Buzz," he began, "I first hired you back in 1946 as a speech writer. We were focused on my 1948 Senate race. I felt from the very beginning that you felt and thought like me. You were the one person on my staff that served as my other self. You've known me as a Congressman, Senator, Majority Leader, Vice President, and now President. I know there have been times that you liked me and disliked me; respected me and disrespected me. Sometimes my public performances clicked, and, other times, I was monumentally boring. You've traveled with me, campaigned with me, laughed with me, worried with me, and shared with me moments of greatest consequence---and moments of complete unimportance. You know me better than any man alive...This November is the pivotal moment in my life. I will be running for the first time on my own for the highest office of the land, the most powerful person perhaps on the globe. This time I am not moving into an office out of tragedy, but on the strength of my own performance, hard work and convictions..."

Johnson put his hand on Busby's knee.

"Do you remember, Buzz, when you first came to work for me, I left you a stack of books about Winston Churchill?"

"Yes, sir," Busby said, "I surely do."

"And do you remember what I said to you at that time?"

"You told me, 'Be my Churchill.'"

Johnson broke out into a big smile. The wrinkles in his forehead deepened, and his large ears rose.

"I need you to be my Churchill now," Johnson said. "I have some notes here that I'd like you to finish into a great speech for the Convention---like the one you wrote for me on Memorial Day in 1963 at Gettysburg. I was just a Vice President then, but your words made me feel like a President."

"Thank you, Lyndon," said Busby, his face flushed.

Johnson unfolded a double-sided piece of paper with his hand-written notes, and began reading:

"I want to talk about the golden torch of promise which John Fitzgerald Kennedy set aflame. I want the American people to know that the needs of all can never be met by parties of the few. The needs of all cannot be met by a business party, or a labor party, not by a war party or a peace party, not by a southern party or a northern party. Our deeds will meet our needs only if we are served by a party which serves all our people."

"I want to remind voters that we are in the midst of the largest and the longest period of peacetime prosperity in our history—but that those of us secure in affluence and safe in power, must not turn from the needs of our neighbors. We must extend the hand of compassion and the hand of affection and love to the old, and the sick, and the hungry. Most Americans want a decent home in a decent neighborhood for all. And so do I. Most Americans want an education for every child to the limit of his ability. And so do I. Most Americans want victory in our war against poverty. And so do I.

"I want to assure Americans the strength of our country is greater than any adversary. That it is greater than the combined might of all the nations, in all the wars, in all the history of this planet. And our superiority is growing."

"I want to say that weapons do not make peace. Men make peace. And peace comes not through strength alone, but through wisdom and patience and restraint. But there is no place in today's world for recklessness. We cannot act rashly with the nuclear weapons that could destroy us all. The only course is to make sure that these weapons are never really used at all. This is a dangerous and a difficult world in which we live. There are no easy answers. But I pledge the firmness to defend freedom, the strength to support that firmness, and a constant, patient effort to move the world toward peace instead of war."

"We cannot allow our great purpose as a nation to be endangered by reckless acts of violence. Those who break the law--those who create disorder--whether in the North or the South--must be caught and must be brought to justice. Our nation represents man's first chance to build the Great Society--a nation where every man can find reward in work and satisfaction in the use of his talents."

"The ultimate test of our civilization, the ultimate test of our faithfulness to our past, is not in our goods and is not in our guns. It is in the quality of our people's lives, and in the men and women that we produce. It is not between liberals and conservatives, it is not between party and party, or platform and platform. It is between courage and timidity. It is between those who have vision--those who see what can be---and those who want only to maintain the status quo. It is between those who welcome the future and those who turn away from its promises."

Johnson put his paper down and looked into Busby's eyes.

"Buzz, I want you to write me a Churchill speech. Valenti helped me put down some notes on this first draft—but you are the only one I can trust to give me a final version that will capture the American spirit."

"Thank you, Mr. President," said Busby, as the President put the papers in his hand.

Johnson held onto Busby's hand and fixed his eyes on Busby, speaking slowly, and with evident emotion:

"This man Goldwater is a cancer on America, Buzz. I'm not only going to beat him in November—I'm going to crush him. I want the landslide on election day to bury Goldwater and Miller so deep---their bodies will never be found. I have not worked this hard for all these years to let our nation slip into the hands of these radical fanatics. And if they *are* remembered at all--I want them to be remembered as the liars and cowards that they were."

Johnson squeezed Busby's hand, rose up from his chair, folded his newspaper under his arm, and strode out of the Treaty Room, leaving Busby with his coffee and his papers.

Busby remained in the room alone for a few minutes. He opened the papers that President Johnson had left him and smoothed them flat on the historic desk. He thought about John Kennedy signing a peace treaty at this desk. Vice President Lyndon Johnson stood just to his left.

Busby glanced down at the papers Johnson had put in his hands. The headline for the speech was written in large capital letters in the President's child-like scrawl:

"BUILDING THE GREAT SOCIETY"

Post Script:

Lyndon Johnson won the 1964 Presidential election by a landslide, capturing 61% of the vote, which at the time set a record for the highest margin of the popular vote in a Presidential election. Johnson won by nearly 16 million votes. Johnson also coasted past Barry Goldwater in the Electoral

College vote as well, 486 to 52. Johnson won in 44 states, except for Arizona and 5 deep South states: Alabama, Georgia, Louisiana, Mississippi, and South Carolina. Democrats also won commanding majorities in both branches of Congress: a 68-32 majority in the Senate, and a 295-140 majority in the House. This Democratic dominance gave President Johnson a clear path to sign many ground-breaking pieces of federal legislation into law.

Johnson played a key role that same year in passage of The Civil Rights Act, overcoming a Republican filibuster in the Senate that went on for 75 hours before the bill passed. As part of his Great Society "War on Poverty" agenda, Johnson won passage in 1964 of the Economic Opportunity Act, which created Food Stamps, Head Start and Community Action programs, which cut poverty in America in half. The following year, Johnson scored two major health care victories with the passage of Medicare and Medicaid.

But by the beginning of 1967, Johnson's handling of the Vietnam War had lost him the support of a majority of Americans. Efforts to seek peace with the North Vietnamese had gone nowhere, bombing campaigns had produced little results, and Americans killed or wounded had reached almost 70,000. Following the North Vietnamese Tet Offensive, public support for the war and for Johnson hit a new low. By the early spring of 1968, Lyndon Johnson told the nation he was ending the bombing of North Vietnam, and seeking peace talks anywhere, and any time. He also announced that he would not seek a second term as the Democratic nomination for the Presidency.

After leaving the White House in January of 1969, Johnson returned to his ranch in Stonewall, Texas. He remained active in Democratic politics, and supported South Dakota Senator George McGovern in the 1972 election. In January of 1973, four years after leaving office, Johnson suffered a major heart attack, and died in his bedroom at the age of 64.

Horace Busby had negotiated with Lyndon Johnson that he would stay with the President only up to the 1964 elections. But Johnson prevailed upon Busby to stay on for a few more months. Busby left the White House in the Fall of 1965 and ended his government service. Johnson sent Busby a letter which read: "As a counselor, you have been wise. As an administrator, you *have been unsparing toward yourself. As a friend, you have been, and you are, a never-failing source of strength to me."*

Returning to the private sector, Busby continued as a political consultant for corporate clients like American Airlines and Mobil Oil.

In 1968, Johnson asked Busby to work on one more speech for him, announcing his intention to drop out of the Presidential race.

Throughout much of his career Busby wrote political newsletters, including the Busby Papers, which he produced from the early 1980s until he retired. Busby correctly predicted that the Republicans would win the 1980 Presidential election because they tightly controlled the South and the Western states.

In 1997, Busby moved to Santa Monica, California. Three years after moving to the Golden State, Busby died of respiratory failure in Santa Monica at the age of 76.

RAILROAD ARMY

In the middle of a bitter and costly coalminer's strike led by labor leader John L. Lewis, Harry Truman had no patience left to deal with a threatened railroad strike.

On Friday, May 17, 1946, one day ahead of the planned massive railroad workers' walk-out, he summoned the head of two railroad workers' unions to meet with him in the White House.

Alexander Whitney, head of the Brotherhood of Railroad Trainmen, and Alvanley Johnston, leader of the Brotherhood of Locomotive Engineers, had a joint audience with the President. Both men were long-time supporters of Truman, going back to his campaign for the Senate in 1940. They also raised most of his campaign funds in 1944 to help Truman at the Chicago Democratic Convention win the Vice Presidential slot on the FDR ticket. Both men considered Truman to be a personal friend and ally over years of political battles.

Truman, dressed in a blue, double-breasted suit, neatly pressed, welcomed his two old friends into the Oval Office, but his tone from the start was anything but friendly.

"You both have no doubt heard the jokes that are being made at my expense," the President began. "'To err is Truman.' And: 'I'm just mild about Harry.' It seems you boys have made me somewhat of a laughing stock in this town..."

Neither Johnston nor Whitney responded." Mr. President," Johnston began— but Truman put up one hand to stop him.

"Let me get right to the issue," the President said. "I am working on a radio speech that I intend to give to the American people a few days from now. I thought you'd like to hear what I'm planning to say..."

"Just understand that our men are demanding a strike," Whitney shot back. "More than 200,000 trainmen have told me what they want me to do. I'm tied to the tracks on this one."

"And I've got 80,000 locomotive engineers," Johnston added. "They want you to know that this train has already left the station."

 Truman brushed off both comments and continued. "I'm going to tell the American people that I brought you both in here 4 months ago to try and avert a strike. I'm going to say that you both flat out refused to meet with the operators and the other 18 unions. You agreed to meet with the operators—but not with the other unions around—so we have to set up three conferences in the White House."

"The operators and the other unions all agreed to take an 18.5 cent raise. They placed the interests of America first. But this compromise was rejected by the locomotive engineers and the trainmen."

"For good reason," Whitney interjected. "They didn't like the terms."

"The terms were eminently fair," Truman mocked. "Your people would have seen an actual increase in their take-home pay---above the greatest take-home pay which they enjoyed during the war. Your members are among the highest paid unions in the country!"

"More upward pressure on wages is needed," Johnston replied. "Don't use other agreements to drag us down. These are working people who vote Truman, who helped you get into this high office."

"I want the American people to know that Mr. Johnston and Mr. Whitney chose to call a strike instead of a settlement. That you knew the terrible havoc this decision would cause and the extreme suffering that will result from a strike. I don't believe that your rank and file realize the terrifying situation created by your actions."

Truman grabbed a heavy glass paperweight from his desk and held it up.

"Your hard-headed actions will lead to a lack of fuel, raw materials and shipping. Hundreds of factories will shut down. Lack of transportation will create chaos in food distribution. When the wives of your members go to the grocery stores, they will find empty shelves. You will see your food supplies dwindle, your health and safety endangered, and your streets darkened. Millions of workers will be thrown out of their jobs. The drop in production will add to our inflationary pressures. All of this is going to come crashing down on your heads, gentlemen."

Truman slammed the paperweight down on his desk.

"And our members will have our heads if we don't keep the pressure on to raise wages, Harry," Whitney said. "You seem to have lost touch with what the working man is going through."

"Your members are going to pay a heavy price for your obstinance," Truman declared. "I'm going to pay a visit to Congress soon, and I'm going to tell them that unless the railroads are manned by returning strikers I will immediately undertake to run them using the Army of the United States! And I will order that all striking members be drafted into the Army."

Both union heads were speechless for several heartbeats. They glanced aside to one another, and then Whitney, who knew the President better, spoke first.

"What? You're going to conscript our members into the Army? That's crazy! You don't have the power to do that!"

"We will hit your Army plan with an injunction," Johnston threatened. "There will be riots in the streets. You can't possibly be serious."

"I assure you," Truman said, "I do not take this action lightly. But there is no alternative. This is no longer a dispute between labor and management. It has now become a strike against the Government of the United States itself. This kind of strike can never be tolerated. If allowed to continue, the government will break down. Strikes against the government must stop."

All three men just looked across the Presidential desk at each other, their internal thoughts too unspeakable. For the labor leaders, this was not the Harry Truman they had come to rely on.

In Chicago in 1944, Johnston and Whitney had campaigned tirelessly to make Harry Truman the vice-presidential candidate in Franklin Delano Roosevelt's reelection campaign. Johnston knew that Truman was closer to Whitney, and that the President referred to Johnston as "that damned Republican." These were the spoils of politics. Johnston openly endorsed Thomas Dewey for President in 1944 because he liked Dewey's welfare plans.

At the close of 1945, the railroad unions were pushing hard for pay increases and a forty-hour work week. Some of the unions began softening their demands, but Johnston and Whitney called the Engineers and Trainmen out on strike in March of 1946. President Truman set up a board to hear the grievances but discussions had not gone well. Between Whitney and Johnston, they represented 289,000 workers. With good reason, Truman feared a railroad strike could paralyze the nation. He felt all the labor leaders had broken their promises to him. "They all lied to me," Truman complained.

"In all my days," Whitney began telling the President, speaking in a slow, measured tone, "I have never heard a more absurd proposal from your lips. I will tell our members that you have totally lost your senses."

Truman stiffened. "We *will* draft them---and think about the law later," he said, with resignation in his voice. "This is a time for plain speaking. I will tell the people that this is not a labor versus management fight. I will say this is a contest between two willful men and their government. I will say 'I am a friend of labor—but it is inconceivable that in a democracy, any two men should be placed in a position where they can completely stifle our economy, and ultimately destroy our country."

Johnston and Whitney both instantly rose to their feet, which caused Truman to rise as well. "I think this conversation is over," Whitney said. "I am truly sorry to part on such terms. You can blame us if you want, Harry, but history will blame you in the end. This is edging toward lunacy."

Truman then slid over a piece of paper that had been lying on his desk. In front of Johnston and Whitney, Truman signed the order, and passed it over to his guests to read. It was an Executive Order that allowed the government to seize and operate the railroads effective the next day.

Johnston and Whitney, still standing, read the order, and put it back down on the desk.

There were no handshakes as Johnston and Whitney showed themselves out of the Oval Office.

Less than 24 hours later, on the Saturday of the planned walkout, Johnston and Whitney sent word back to the White House that they were agreeable to postpone the strike for five more days.

On the third day of the strike extension, Truman formally proposed giving the railroad workers an 18.5 cent raise, but Whitney and Johnston said they were still "unfavorably" disposed to the plan.

On the final day of the postponement, Truman wrote the draft of a long speech in which he railed against his old friends—Whitney and Johnston---who had not only defied the President's office but had belittled him personally. He noted that these "effete union leaders" were earning five to ten times the salary that he made as President. "I am tired of the government being flouted, vilified, and misrepresented," Truman wrote. He suggested that some union leaders were communists, and that it was time "to give the country back to the people...and tell the Russians where to get off."

The next evening, May 24th, Truman gave his scheduled radio address to the public. He called on the striking railroad workers to go back to their jobs, and said if they did not, he would call in the Army and take whatever measures needed to end the strike.

The following afternoon, the President delivered his speech to Congress.

"Strikes against the government must stop." Truman said. "What we are dealing with here is not labor as a whole. We are dealing with a handful of men who are striking against their own government and against every one of their fellow citizens, and against themselves. We are dealing with a handful of men who have it within their power to cripple to entire economy of the nation."

"I request temporary legislation to take care of this immediate crisis." Truman added. "I request permanent legislation leading to the formulation of a long-range labor policy designed to prevent the recurrence of such crises and generally to reduce the stoppages of work in all industries for the future...This legislation must be used in a way that is fair to capital and labor alike. The President will not permit either side—industry or workers—to use it to further their own selfish interests or to foist upon the government the carrying out of their selfish aims."

Even as the President was delivering his speech, the Assistant to the President, John Roy Steelman, was negotiating with Whitney and Johnston in their room at the Statler Hotel. When Truman got to the part of his text where we said he would ask Congress to pass a "temporary emergency" law which allowed him to draft striking railroad workers into the Army, the Secretary of the Senate handed Truman a red note.

Truman stopped, read the short note, and then diverted from his text. "Word has just been received," the President announced, "that the railroad strike has been settled, on terms proposed by the President!" The entire Congress rose to its feet to applaud the announcement.

The President's proposed legislation to draft striking railworkers into the Army passed overwhelmingly in the U.S. House 306 to 13, but was killed by liberal Democrats in the Senate, who doubted the measure's constitutionality.

After the Senate vote to kill the Railroad Army, Whitney told his secretary to set up a meeting as soon as possible between himself, Alvanley Johnston, and Commerce Secretary Henry Wallace. "Tell Secretary Wallace I want to chat with him about his thoughts on the guaranteed annual minimum wage for all workers," Whitney said. "Tell him, Labor has 'Had it with Harry.' Tell him, 'Alexander Whitney wants to hear more about this Progressive Party idea of his.'"

"By the hand of God," Whitney said. "I'll go with Dewey in '48 if I have to. Harry can go back to that haberdashery shop in Missouri. Let him recruit the goddamn Army to help him sell hatbands."

President Truman told his friends at a private dinner party at the White House that he felt like he was standing on the tracks as a runaway locomotive barreled down on him. "I was the servant of 150 million people of the United States, and I had to do the job even if I lost my political career."

At a labor rally a few days later in Madison Square Park in Manhattan, Alexander Whitney announced that President Truman's actions had amounted to signing his own political death certificate. "You can't make a President Out of a ribbon clerk," he told the crowd. "I promise you today that I will spend every penny in the treasury of the Brotherhood of Railroad Trainmen that strikebreaker Harry Truman will not become President in 1948."

Post Script:

The railroad confrontations with the White House were just one of Harry Truman's ongoing confrontations with organized labor. In the spring of

1947, Congress put on his desk the Taft-Hartley Act, which was viewed as a measure to curtail the power of labor unions. Truman, despite his frustration with the unions, vetoed the bill, and Congress overrode his veto. But Truman used his veto in the run-up to the 1948 election, promising labor activists that he would work to repeal Taft-Hartley.

In the presidential election of that year, Truman sought to push civil rights reforms as an issue, alienating many Democratic supporters from the South. He attacked Republicans, whom he said "think the American standard of living is a fine thing—so long as it doesn't spread to all the people." As the election neared, the Democratic party appeared to be fractured: a splinter group of Southern Democrats formed a "Dixiecrat" ticket, and a left wing "Progressive Party" got on the ballot, headed by former Vice President Henry Wallace, who advocated for national health insurance and voting rights for Blacks.

To bring his message to the people, Harry Truman conducted an exhausting "whistle stop" train campaign across the country. Republican candidate Thomas Dewey was widely predicted to win the race, but on election day, Truman won 303 electoral votes to Dewey's 189. The Dixiecrats won 39 electoral votes, and Progressive Henry Wallace won no electoral votes.

In 1950, Truman survived an assassination attempt carried out by two Puerto Rican nationalists. At the time, Truman was living at the Blair House, while the White House was undergoing extensive renovations.

In 1952, Truman's labor policies again were in the headlines, as the President sought to take control over a number of prominent steel mills, to ensure steel was available for the war effort in Korea. The U.S. Supreme Court ruled Truman's plan unconstitutional, saying that the President had no executive authority to commandeer the mills---just as he likely had no authority to draft railroad workers into the Army.

By 1952, Truman's popularity was again on the wane, and instead of running for a second term, he lobbied Adlai Stevenson, the Governor of Illinois, to seek the nomination at the Democratic National Convention. Stevenson won the nomination but was soundly defeated by Republican Dwight Eisenhower in the November election.

After leaving the White House, Truman returned to his home in Independence, Missouri. He was offered a book deal for his memoirs, which *he divided into two parts:* Memoirs by Harry S. Truman: Year of Decisions and Memoirs by Harry S. Truman: Years of Trial and Hope. *This two-volume memoir was published in 1955 and 1956 and was a commercial and critical success.*

Truman supported Adlai Stevenson in a second, unsuccessful, bid for the White House in 1956. In 1965, President Lyndon Johnson came to the Truman Library to sign the newly-enacted Medicare law and gave the first two Medicare cards to Truman and his wife Bess to honor the former president's advocacy for government health care while he was in the White House.

At the close of 1972, Truman died at the age of 88 from complications of pneumonia.

After the 1946 railroad strike, Alexander Whitney told his members that he planned to muster the union's financial power to defeat Harry Truman at the polls. Whitney was considering putting his support behind Henry Wallace's Progressive Party, but Whitney decided that Wallace was too far to the left, and that a Third-Party candidate was not viable.

In 1947, Whitney mended fences with Truman over the Taft-Hartley Act. When Truman vetoed the anti-labor bill, Whitney told railroad workers that Truman had "vindicated himself in the eyes of labor." Whitney pledged the full support of his Brotherhood of Railroad Trainmen to Truman's candidacy.

Alexander Whitney died of a heart attack in the summer of 1949 at the age of 76.

Alvanley Johnston retired from the Brotherhood of Locomotive Engineers in 1950. He died in the Fall of 1951 at the age of 76.

JAPANESE WORK CORPS

On February 5, 1942, roughly two months after the bombing of Pearl Harbor by Japan, the director of the U.S. Office of Naval Intelligence (ONI), Rear Admiral Walter Stratton Anderson, held a confidential briefing for key ONI staff on the fifth floor of the Van Nuys Building at the office of the Eleventh Naval District in Los Angeles. The meeting was conducted by Kenneth Ringle, the assistant district intelligence officer for ONI's Eleventh District.

Given the imminent establishment of internment camps for Japanese living in America, the ONI was accelerating its efforts to create a coherent policy about how to deal with the Japanese on the West Coast.

Officer Ringle, who was bilingual in Japanese, had travelled extensively up and down the west coast after Pearl Harbor, and had developed a network of Japanese American informants. He had also conducted a raid on the Japanese consulate in Los Angeles that led to the dissolution of a Japanese spy ring.

An invitation had been extended by Ringle to Curtis B. Munson, a Detroit businessman commissioned as a special representative of the State Department, to present a report he had submitted to ONI in November of 1941 entitled "Japanese on the West Coast."

At 10 am Pacific time, Ringle began the meeting by introducing Mr. Munson:

"Gentlemen, thank you all so much for joining our ONI team this morning for a backgrounder on the status of Japanese Americans on the west coast. I have coded this briefing as 'confidential'—so please observe the standard ONI protocols for this meeting.

"As you know, in roughly two weeks President Roosevelt is expected to sign an Executive Order that will authorize the evacuation of Japanese persons—both alien and non-alien—from many parts of the Western Defense Command. Heads of household will be instructed to report to the nearest Civil Control Station by April 2nd to await further instructions. Japanese persons will be provided with temporary residence elsewhere, and with services with respect to the management, leasing, storage or other disposition of most kinds of property, including real estate, business and professional equipment, buildings, household goods, boats, automobiles, livestock, etc.

"Many of you may have reviewed the summary of Mr. Curtis B. Munson's report to ONI on this topic. To prepare his report, Mr. Munson toured California and the Pacific Coast, interviewing Army and Marine intelligence officers, the FBI, military commanders, and city officials. His Report has been reviewed by Secretary of War Stimson, Secretary of the Navy Knox, Attorney General Biddle, and Secretary of State Hull. After Mr. Munson's remarks, I shall add some comments of my own."

"So, without further introduction, please welcome Curtis B. Munson."

Munson took his place behind a wooden lectern and lay down his briefing papers beneath the small light.

"Thank you, Commander, for those introductory comments," Munson said, adjusting the light to the page. "I appreciate the opportunity to present my report, which I originally submitted in early November of 1941, titled simply: 'Japanese on the West Coast.' I gave my report to John Franklin Carter at White House intelligence, who in turn shared them directly with the President."

"I spent about a week each in the 11th, 12th and 13th Naval Districts with the full cooperation of the Naval and Army intelligences and the FBI. Our Navy has done by far the most work on this problem, having given it intense consideration for the last ten or fifteen years."

"Let me summarize my findings by saying first: there are still Japanese in the United States who will tie dynamite around their waist and make a human bomb out of themselves---but today they are few. Second, there is no Japanese 'problem' on the coast. There will be no armed uprising of Japanese. There will be undoubtedly some sabotage financed by Japan and executed largely by imported agents. There will be the odd case of fanatical sabotage by some Japanese 'crackpot.' The dangerous part of their espionage is that they would be very effective as far as movement of supplies, movement of troops and movement of ships is concerned. But for the most part, the local Japanese are loyal to the United States or, at worst, they hope that by remaining quiet they can avoid concentration camps or irresponsible mobs."

"An American wit once said, 'You cannot tell the truth about Japan without lying.' This same might be made with reference to the Japanese people. The Japanese are a perplexing people and their study is a very interesting and very enlightening one. They follow the leader – they have done this throughout all the years of their history. Even today, personal ties are stronger than legal ones. There are several divisions of Japanese in the United States. Suffice it to say that Japanese family life is disciplined and honorable. The children are obedient and the girls virtuous. The Japanese is the greatest joiner in the world. To take care of this passion, he has furnished himself with ample Associations to join. There are around 1,563 of these Japanese Associations in the United States."

"The First Generation Japanese are considerably weakened in their loyalty to Japan by the fact that they have chosen to make America their home and have brought up their children here. They expect to die here. They are quite fearful of being put in a concentration camp. Many would take out American citizenship if allowed to do so. They are also still legally Japanese. Yet they do break with Japan and send their boys off to the Army with pride and tears.

"They are good neighbors. They are old men fifty-five to sixty-five, for the most part simple and dignified. They were Japanese lower middle class about analogous to the pilgrim fathers. They were largely farmers and fishermen. Today the Japanese is farmer, fisherman and businessman. They get very attached to the land they work or own, they like their own business, they do not work at industrial jobs, nor for others---except as a stepping stone to becoming independent."

"Second Generation Japanese, age 1 to 30 years, who have received their whole education in the United States and usually, in spite of discrimination against them and a certain amount of insults accumulated through the years from irresponsible elements, show a pathetic eagerness to be Americans. They are estimated from 90% to 98% loyal to the United States. They are not Japanese in culture. They are foreigners to Japan. Though

American citizens, they are not accepted by Americans, because they look differently and can be easily recognized. These Second generation Japanese hardly know where to turn. Some gesture of protection or wholehearted acceptance of this group would go a long way to swinging them away from any last romantic hankering after old Japan."

"They are not oriental or mysterious, they are very American and are a proud, self-respecting race suffering from a little inferiority complex and a lack of contact with the white boys they went to school with. They are eager for this contact and to work alongside them."

"Those American-born Japanese who received part or all of their education in Japan, and who received their education in Japan from childhood to about age 17–and those who received their early education in the U.S. but who returned to Japan for 4 or 5 years of Japanese education---these are considered the most dangerous element."

"In each Naval District there are about 250 to 300 suspects under surveillance. The Intelligence Services believe that only 50 or 60 in each district can be classed as really dangerous. The Japanese are hampered as saboteurs because of their easily recognized physical appearance. It will be hard for them to get near anything to blow up if it is guarded. There is far more danger from Communists than there is from Japanese. The Japanese here is almost exclusively a farmer, a fisherman or a small business man."

Munson reached over for a small glass of water, took a sip, set the glass down, and returned to his report.

"There will be no wholehearted response from Japanese in the United States regarding sabotage. They will be in a position to pick up information on troop, supply and ship movements from local Japanese, but for the most part the local Japanese are loyal to the United States. We do not believe that they would be any more disloyal than any other racial group in the United States with whom we went to war."

"The Navy or some unified authority should have complete control of the harbor of Los Angeles before the outbreak of war with Japan. That time is now. The Japanese are loyal on the whole, but we are wide open to sabotage on this Coast and as far inland as the mountains, and while this one fact goes unrectified, I cannot unqualifiedly state that there is no danger from the Japanese living in the United States."

"After submitting my report to John Carter, I told him that I was aware of at least 5 Japanese-Americans in Los Angeles who had committed suicide because they loyalty to America was under suspicion. I told Mr. Carter it was essential to use Japanese filial piety as hostage for good behavior. I urged him to review Commander Ringle's proposal for maintaining the loyalty of Japanese-Americans and establishing wholesome races relations. I will now let Commander Ringle pick up the story from here..."

Lieutenant Commander Kenneth Ringle then took his place at the lectern. He was slightly taller than Curtis Munson, and was more formally dressed in his pressed Navy uniform and Commander's cap.

"Thank you, Curtis, for your excellent background report. I believe all of you know that on 26 January I submitted a confidential report to the Chief of Naval Operations entitled a 'Report on the Japanese Question.' My conclusions about the 'Japanese threat' are very similar to Mr. Munson's."

"The alien menace is becoming of less importance almost daily, as the original Japanese immigrants grow older and die, and as more and more of their American-born children reach maturity. Of those American-born United States citizens of Japanese ancestry, it is considered that least 75% are loyal to the United States. The large majority are at least passively loyal to the United States. They would knowingly do nothing whatever to the injury of the United States---but at the same time---would not do anything to the injury of Japan."

"Most of these Japanese will not engage in active sabotage or insurrection--- but they might well do surreptitious observation work for Japanese interests if given a convenient opportunity. I estimate that there are some Japanese who would act as saboteurs or agents—but this number is less than three per cent of the total, or about 3,500 in the entire United States."

"The most potentially dangerous element of all are the Kibei, those American citizens of Japanese ancestry who have spent the formative years of their lives, from 10 to 20, in Japan and have returned to the United States within the last few years. These people are essentially and inherently

Japanese and may have been deliberately sent back to the United States by the Japanese government to act as agents. These Kibei should be looked upon as enemy aliens and many of them placed in custodial detention. This group numbers between 600 and 700 in the Los Angeles metropolitan area."

"These enemy aliens should be physically separated from the balance of the Japanese and should be guarded both for the protection of the United States and for their own physical protection. A reversal of the commonly accepted legal procedure must be exercised, for the best interests of the United States, with persons considered guilty unless proven innocent. They must be able to prove beyond a reasonable doubt that they are not potentially dangerous. They should not be allowed employment in private industry or membership in the War Relocation Work Corps. At the first opportunity, or at the conclusion of the present war, they should be deported to Japan, and their status as legal residents of the United States or as citizens of the United States canceled."

"Any person desiring to announce himself as a loyal citizen of Japan may do so without fear or prejudice, irrespective of whether or not he holds American citizenship. If they so desire, they will be exchanged for American citizens held by the Japanese Government. As soon as possible after the conclusion of hostilities they will be repatriated to Japan."

"I have developed a proposal for a 'War Relocation Work Corps,' set up on the basis of desirability and on an appeal to patriotism. The evacuees should be made to feel that any true American-faced with a similar situation-would instantly want to seize the opportunity to enlist and to perform the essential war work which it is presumed that the Corps will do."

"The Work Corps would be primarily a project for American citizens—but loyal aliens would be welcomed. Enlistment would be voluntary. However, all the benefits of work---tangible and intangible---such as wages, furloughs, share in the profits of community enterprises, service records and discharge, the holding of any executive or administrative position under the Authority, are to be reserved for members of the Work Corps. An enlistee should occupy a position analogous to the breadwinner of a family, so that no penalty or stigma will be attached to dependents of such enlistee should they elect not to join."

"The Work Corps could have a system of service records and various types of discharges. Upon completion of enlistment in the Corps, the enlistee could be given one of a number of classes of discharge, depending upon his performance of duty with the Corps: bad conduct, ordinary, honorable, honorable with credit, honorable with special credit. The service record and discharge then would become a most valuable reference in seeking employment in private industry or as a document attesting to character. A battalion system would provide for the division into technical skills, with the engineers' battalion, the agricultural battalion, the service battalion, the medical and nursing battalion, and the like."

"As to insignia, there should be some sort of cloth device, sewn into a shirt or jacket on the point of the shoulder, similar to the Army's division insignia, which could designate the Work Corps and possibly the relocation center in which organized. On the breast could be another device showing the battalion, and the various grades or ratings could easily be shown by a system of horizontal or diagonal short stripes on the arm as is now done in both Army and Navy for non-commissioned grades."

"The choice of individual designs could well be left to a contest in design by the evacuees themselves. If the separate design on the breast of the garment seems superfluous, an adaptation of the Navy system, in which a basic design shows the specialty---boatswains mate, coppersmith, machinist, or merely deck and engineer ratings---could be used, consolidated with the stripes showing rating, the whole to be placed on the arm. The cloth is suggested so that the badges would be equally effective on a shirt, jacket, women's blouse, windbreaker, or cold weather clothing."

"This would be cheap, could be manufactured by the Japanese evacuee women themselves on the project. Most Japanese girls are extremely skillful needle women and excel most white women in skill with the sewing machine. The Japanese have an infinite capacity for taking pains and an infinite patience which qualifies them for detailed work even though it may be monotonous in character."

"If heads of families elect not to join, they would not be permitted to work on center or community projects, would not be eligible for furloughs, or for private employment off the project. However, they will be housed and fed and will be allowed $5 per month per family cash allowance. This allowance is not wages in any sense of the word but falls in the category of a 'health and comfort' allowance and is for the purchase of such necessities as soap, tooth paste, razor blades, articles of clothing, and the like."

"The evacuees will certainly not be displacing other labor and will perform a very necessary task. Some white American official of the War Relocation Authority would take charge of two or three companies of volunteer evacuees into such a center of agriculture, and solicit applications from farmers who need harvest help, making all arrangements as to wages, subsistence and lodging, receiving all moneys, etc. The harvest could be followed as far as the Canadian border, at which time the group could return to its center. Conveyance could be by truck, housing in Army tents, subsistence by rolling kitchens, if so desired."

"The War Relocation Authority can do a very good job of Americanization within relocation centers. They will offer a free flow of American newspapers, magazines, books, etc., into the communities. They can establish a movie theater in each community and setting up a movie exchange circuit through the centers, showing not only Hollywood's efforts in entertainment, but American newsreels, educational programs, films such as the *March of Time*, and others of a like nature. We can arrange speaking, lecturing and entertainment tours by American groups. We can recruit as many trained Caucasian American teachers in the schools as it is possible to obtain with the money available. We can arrange personal appearances or addresses by notables in American life, including if possible, some of our military and naval heroes. And finally, we can help these Japanese acquire the attitude that as a matter of course they are loyal Americans, and that we naturally expect them to live up to our expectations."

"I have no objection to staging Japanese folk dances, classes in Japanese flower arrangement, or other purely artistic or cultural pursuits—as long as the camp authorities are satisfied the activity is purely artistic or cultural in nature. After all, the Japanese have a culture and art that is recognized all over the world. Would you forbid the waltz because of the German origin of much of its music? Or ban the production of an opera because its original composer was Italian?"

"I would allow the inhabitants of a project to decide what type of youth organizations they desire or need. The Authority should help them to set up such American organizations as the Boy Scouts, Girl Scouts, YWCA, YMCA, or any others which conform to the generally accepted pattern of those normally found in any American community. This is in line with my suggestion of calmly assuming that these people desire to follow accepted American standards. I see no reason for excluding Buddhism as a religion from the camps---but I would most certainly go over every Buddhist priest with a fine-tooth comb and exclude everyone about whom there was the slightest doubt---particularly if that priest were an alien who had either entered the country originally since about 1933, or who had made extended or numerous trips to Japan since that time."

"If the Buddhist congregations are left without priests by such a course of action, that is too bad. Also, I would insist that religious services be conducted in the English language wherever possible. Shintoism is a horse of another color. It is the official Japanese state religion: the Emperor of Japan is at once the high priest and the object of worship along with the imperial ancestors. It is not a true religion---but a form of patriotism toward Japan. I do not see how it can possibly be allowed."

"If we can assure the American public that persons permitted to accept private employment or to be members of the War Relocation Work Corps are only those considered non-dangerous, I believe much of the hysterical resentment against these people would disappear and that work opportunities and resettlement opportunities would be easier to obtain. We need to proceed with the calm assumption that these people are American in spirit---even if all are not citizens---and that therefore they will wish to conform to American ideas and standards of behavior."

"The Japanese have an intense dislike of ridicule. This characteristic can be used by pointing out to them that a certain attitude is laughable – 'Look at so and so. He is making a perfect laughing stock of himself by his attitude and behavior.'"

With that, Commander Ringle stepped away from lectern, and softly clicked off the lectern lamp.

"Let me pause here and accept a few questions you might have..." Ringle said.

One hand rose in the back of the room: "Commander, is there a way to reward internees who turn in subversives among their group? Like a special insignia on their uniform?"

Ringle stepped back into the microphone. "Off-hand I would see certain challenges in that approach," he said, "since no one will want to be identified as our agent against their own people—but let me take your question under advisement. Any other questions, or comments?"

"Yes, Commander," said one man who appeared to be an intelligence staffer in civilian clothes: "Do you think the Japanese is being singled out for these camps because he is yellow? Don't we have similar concerns for Italian or German saboteurs?"

"I think there is some truth to that. Unfortunately, the Japanese can be easily identified by his skin color, whereas you can't know for sure who is an Italian or a German until he opens his mouth. As Curtis Munson and I have stated, we did not recommend to President Roosevelt that internment camps were advisable in the first place. But our recommendations fell on deaf ears in the White House. So, I turned to the Work Camp idea to try and create a higher degree of loyalty to America among the Japanese population. I hope we will be able to demonstrate that assertive persuasion will go farther than ruthless persecution."

With that, Ringle glanced at this watch, and turned to his men with a final comment:

"On behalf of Curtis Munson and myself, let me leave you with this thought: Because these people have Oriental faces, it is natural to look for and probably stress the differences between them and Caucasian Americans. This I believe is wrong. The points of similarity should be stressed. If this point of view is taken, I believe the intelligent observer will be amazed at how little different basically these people are from their American contemporaries."

"Within the present decade, from 1940 to 1950, there will be a complete and sharp shifting of leadership and power – political, economic, cultural, religious, and social – from the older Japanese-born generation to the younger American born and reared generation. Whether the younger generations become truly American in thought, word, deed, and sentiment will depend on the way in which they are treated now, and on how they are helped to meet the test of this war."

"I believe that whether or not we have a 'Yellow Problem' in the United States for the next hundred and fifty years will be decided by the attitude of the United States as a whole to the Japanese-Americans before 1950. It is preferable that we assimilate these yellow races now, rather than isolate them later."

"Someday you will walk right past a Japanese and not think twice about it."

Post Script:

Kenneth Ringle's report and recommendations were submitted to the Office of Naval Intelligence. But the Army moved forward with its plans for mass internment of Japanese-Americans. Ringle's work was filed away and never implemented. Ringle continued to push his plans with John Franklin Carter, who was in charge of President Roosevelt's own group of secret agents. Ringle proposed that trusted Japanese-Americans be allowed to have supervision over other Japanese considered less trustworthy. Despite apparent agreement from President Roosevelt, Ringle was unable to get the Army to meet with him to discuss his proposals. Lt. Gen. J.L. Dewitt, the Army officer charged with defending the West Coast, did not believe in categorizing Japanese Americans based on their level of loyalty. He once commented, "A Jap is a Jap."

When mass internment became a reality, Ringle felt like he had been an accomplice to the betrayal of Japanese-Americans.

Ringle worked for a short time for the War Relocation Authority in 1942, elaborating his idea that the most threatening Japanese could be separated out of the camps, and others in the camps could be resettled back into a normal environment.

As World War II progressed, Ringle served combat duty on board the USS Honolulu, and later as commanding officer of the USS Wasatch in 1945. He was awarded a Legion of Merit for his engagement in the Battle of Leyte Gulf.

Ringle believed that his reports on the Japanese situation had harmed his Naval career, because his work was kept secret and it distracted him from his core naval career. After the war, Ringle was the commander of a transport ship division in China.

Ringle retired from the Navy in 1953 with a promotion from Captain to Rear Admiral. He died of a heart attack in 1963 while living in Louisiana. He was 63 years old.

Curtis Munson had been hired as an agent reporting directly to John Franklin Carter on President Roosevelt's staff. Following Munson's West Coast investigations, he went on to Hawaii to continue his work. His investigations in Hawaii reflected the same conclusions as his West Coast study.

After the attack on Pearl Harbor, Munson continued to send additional reports to Carter for a couple of months. Munson told Roosevelt that the attack on Pearl Harbor was the work of Japanese nationals, not Japanese American agents. He said Pearl Harbor was "the proof of the pudding" of his report's conclusion that Japanese-Americans were no security threat.

Curtis B. Munson, in agreement with Kenneth Ringle, developed a policy for President Roosevelt that suggested the second-generation Japanese-Americans, known as the "Nisei," should be given the responsibility of keeping track of other Japanese in America. The Nisei were defined as Japanese age one to 30 years who had received all of their education in the United States and who showed "a pathetic eagerness to be Americans," according to Munson. The theory was that the Nisei would transfer control from the Japanese nationals to the more loyal Nisei, who were American citizens. The Nisei would police their parents.

Munson's finding in December of 1941 that five Japanese Americans in Los Angeles had committed suicide because their honor was questioned over suspicions of their loyalty to America was sent to Roosevelt, along with Ringle's plan for fostering better race relations with the Japanese Americans. The President passed along Munson's recommendations to J. Edgar Hoover and Attorney General, both of whom were supportive, according to Carter.

But after Pearl Harbor, the Army asked for the authority over all "aliens" on the west coast. Munson sent a letter to Roosevelt just before Christmas of 1941, informing the President that "99% of the most intelligent views on the Japanese by military, official and civil contacts on the West Coast and Hawaii" agreed with the assessment of Kenneth Ringle. But my mid-February of 1942, the War Department had given the Army a Presidential order empowering them to remove American citizens who were of Japanese ancestry, as well as those who "aliens," from the West Coast.

Munson wrote later that month: "We are drifting into a treatment of the Japanese corresponding to Hitler's treatment of the Jews." Nearly 112,000 people of Japanese ancestry were interned in camps.

During World War II, Munson took part in American landings in Africa and Italy. He was at Omaha Beach in Normandy.

After the War, Munson pursued business ventures in Canada. A native of Washington, D.C. Munson died in 1980 of a stroke. He was 88 years old. His obituary did not mention at all his work for President Roosevelt regarding the Japanese on the West Coast.

CHINA OPENED

"Is the President of the United States supposed to hitchhike to Chairman Mao's house?"

Henry Kissinger put down his copy of the *Washington Post*, and glanced over at Colonel Al Haig, who sat across from his desk in the basement office of the Assistant to the President for National Security Affairs. Kissinger had raised his eyebrows with an expression of incredulity.

It was early February of 1972—just days before the first White House official visit to China.

"Who takes credit for this brilliant piece of advance work?"

"Mr. Secretary," Haig said, "some of our advance men are obsessed with the fact that China is a sovereign state. The Secret Service was not keen on the idea of having Nixon riding in a Chinese car. They said it raised a lot of security challenges."

"I'm sure it does," Kissinger said, "and it raises a host of other problems as well."

"Right. But the Chinese response was they didn't want their people to see the President being driven around in a long, black American limousine with the Presidential seal and plainclothes officers riding the bumper."

"Do they suggest we bring the President in on a rickshaw?" Kissinger laughed.

"Yeah, that would be like a Charlie Chan spoof," Haig noted. "We sat down with some of their people and came up with a compromise."

"What compromise?" Kissinger asked.

"Nixon will use his own armor-plated limousine if he's moving about on his own," Haig said, sweeping his arm in a long motion. "But if he was riding anywhere with Chou En-Lai, he will ride in the Premier's car."

"I don't like the sound of that," Kissinger replied. "Two superpower leaders in one car? I don't like the possibilities that would create for a single terrorist act…"

"I know. We raised that with the Chinese but they said they've done this with the Russians and the British without incident."

"I don't want our President to be the first incident. That kind of logic on their part makes no sense," Kissinger protested. "We can't put all our assets in one box."

He thought for a moment, and then asked: "Did anyone bring up the idea of a body double?"

"Yeah, we did. They were amenable to a decoy limousine, with one of our people inside. We suggested one of those new Dongfeng cars. They were founded last year, as part of Chairman Mao's "Third Front" strategy. The Chinese told us their cars are made in Wuhan."

Kissinger rose from his chair and pulled the floor length curtains back from one window.

"I think," he began, "we should stick with the idea that the President arrives in his own limo, with his own entourage, but that once we start to move throughout China, they we use the Premier's vehicles. Let me work on Nixon about that. He may not like it right off—but he's rightfully more concerned about what to say in Mao's presence---than how he gets to the Imperial Palace."

"Let me check with the Chinese to see what kind of security personnel they will be making available for us, and how these people are screened," Haig said.

"I can ask Wilson Lord to be available to you on this if it would help?"

"Let me get back to you on that, Mr. Secretary."

"There is one other thing," Haig said. "We need to agree on a plan for airplane flights inside China."

"What's the issue?" Kissinger asked.

"The Secret Service was not happy about having the President flying around in Chinese planes. But they didn't feel they could come right out and say that Chinese aircraft are unsafe."

"How about telling them that Nixon always insists on using our planes on every leg of the journey? I think that's not far from the truth. The President does prefer familiar planes. He feels more comfortable knowing who his pilots are, and how his plane is set up. It's not really stretching the truth much."

"The reality," Haig said, "is that if the Secret Service presses on this issue too hard, we might find ourselves unable to fly to any venues inside the country. We'd be relegated to train travel—and that raises all kinds of security alarms. Just think Agatha Christie."

Kissinger smiled. "Please, no Orient Express jokes in front of our hosts."

"Never. I'd never do that."

"Then let's tell our hosts that we will proceed with their plan to have the President in Chinese cars and Chinese planes while he is on the Mainland---but his trip from the airport to the Imperial City will be in the American limousine. But I'd like a briefing book prepared on Chinese security assets from the time we arrive in Shanghai, and take on Chinese navigators, to the time we depart from Peking on the return trip."

"Are we all set on the protocols as we deplane from Air Force One?" Colonel Haig asked.

"Yes," Kissinger replied. "I ran that all by the President. The one detail he was adamant about was not repeating the Dulles gaffe from 1954---when Dulles refused to shake Chou's hand. When Air Force One opens, the President is going to step out alone. I'm supposed to hold everyone else back. The President will descend to the tarmac and shake Chou's hand---Haldeman and I will hold everyone else in the official party back on the plane, until that handshake is done."

"Have we firmed up what's on the agenda—and what's off bounds?" Haig asked his superior.

"Well, Winston has produced excellent briefing books for the President. He's listed out each topic area, and the talking points that the President might care to pursue. All of my meetings with Chou En-Lai are printed out, arranged alphabetically by subject. He's included a long piece on both Chou and Mao that the CIA prepared for us, and a whole addendum of articles and books from China scholars living in the west."

"Has the President seen these briefings yet? Haig wondered.

"*Seen* them," Kissinger said with amusement. "I think the President has *memorized* the talking points. He's got entire passages underlined. By the time he shakes Chou's hand, he'll be able to make a script sound as if he's speaking extemporaneously."

"And what about the visit with Mao?"

"When we get summoned, "Kissinger said, "I will ask Chou if I can bring along Winston Lord. That will be the extent of our group. Winston will be taking notes---but I don't want to irritate folks over at State who will not be able to come."

"They will definitely be irritated," Haig offered. "Can I ask: Is there room for me in that visit?"

"I'm sorry, Al. Both the President and our hosts want the visit with Mao to be very small. I had to get special dispensation from Chou to get Wilson inside."

"I don't have to have any speaking role," Haig pushed back. "I can back up Winston in the note-taking. It's a once in a lifetime opportunity..."

"I know, Al, but we don't set the rules here. I have learned from experience that you never get much advance notice from Mao. On one of my visits with the Chairman, I was told that he wanted to meet my wife, Nancy. One of their protocol officers extracted her from a Peking retail store and brought her to the meeting. It all happened so fast that our agent who was covering Nancy thought she was still shopping. He completely lost track of her. I remember going to Mao's house—which was very simple and unimposing. Our car was able to drive right up to the front door, underneath a portico. It had a small sitting room, which opened into a wider hallway. And in that hallway was a ping pong table."

"A ping pong table? Did Mao play?"

"When I saw him," Kissinger noted, "he had already suffered a series of strokes. Not only was ping pong now beyond his powers, but it took considerable effort to speak. His aides have to write down what he says and show it to him for his approval."

"And all this elaborate preparation to meet with a man who is so compromised, and yet so powerful," Haig marveled.

"The man emanates strength, power, and will," Kissinger said, with a broad note of admiration in his voice. "He is a Colossus of History, created out of a vast People's movement."

"A Colossus with a ping pong table," Haig joked.

"Al, you must keep in mind: every visit to China is a carefully choreographed dance," Kissinger said. It will include planes, and trains and ping pong tables. But note this well: everything will be made to appear spontaneous, but nothing will be done by accident."

"One could argue that the entire sweep of history is fashioned in such a manner,' Kissinger said, returning to his morning newspaper.

"I had hoped I could meet him, shake his hand," Haig said again, with disappointment. "I put as much time into this as Haldeman—and maybe more than Wilson Lord. If I was in charge, I'd let one more person into that room."

"I know you're disappointed, Al," Kissinger consoled him, putting an arm on his shoulder. "And I am sorry. But this is one piece of history we don't get to script."

Colonel Haig just stood there. He made no move to leave.

"I'll bet Mao wouldn't care," he finally said. "He probably knows who I am."

Kissinger picked up his office phone and pushed one of the buttons that was not lit up.

"Can you order two pastrami sandwiches on rye for me and Colonel Haig?

He then turned back to Haig.

"Power is the great aphrodisiac," Kissinger smiled.

Post Script:

President Richard Nixon's 7-day visit to China in 1972 was considered the diplomatic triumph of his Administration. The visit was referred to as the "opening up" of China to the West. The President's meeting with Mao Tse - tung lasted roughly an hour. Alexander Haig was not the only member of the American delegation who was excluded from the meeting with Chairman Mao. William Rogers, Nixon's Secretary of State, was also not invited to the meeting.

The Americans learned later that Mao had been recently hospitalized and was still in poor health leading up to the visit. The conversation during the meeting was described as "casual" and meandered through many topics.

Henry Kissinger made more than 50 visits to China over 4 decades, as a national security adviser, secretary of state, and foreign policy expert. He was awarded a Nobel Peace Prize in 1973, and the Medal of Liberty. He is the chairman of Kissinger Associates, an international consulting firm.

Al Haig was a National Security Advisor to Henry Kissinger at the time of the Nixon visit to China. He was appointed vice chief of staff of the Army, and in 1973, after H.R. Haldeman resigned as Nixon's chief of staff in the wake of the Watergate scandal, Haig became Nixon's Chief of Staff. After Nixon resigned in the summer of 1974, Haig stayed on for a short time as President Gerald Ford's chief of staff, moving on to become the Supreme Allied Commander of all NATO forces in Europe.

Haig retired from the Army in 1979 and the following year President Ronald Reagan nominated Haig to be his secretary of State. After the attempted assassination of Reagan, while the President was in the hospital, Haig made his famous statement, "I am in control here." Haig resigned from Reagan's cabinet in 1982 and ran unsuccessfully for President in the Republican primaries in 1988.

Haig never did have a face to face meeting with Mao Tse-tung, but a year before the Nixon visit to China, Brigadier General Haig met in the Great Hall of the People in Beijing with Chinese Prime Minister Chou En-lai. The Prime Minister opened up that meeting by saying to Haig: "We gave you too much wine today? Our hosts did not know how to make conversation, so they just drowned you in wine."

Mao Tse-tung died from complications of Parkinson's disease on September 9, 1976, at the age of 82, in Beijing, China.

WOOL SHODDIES

"Tariffs do not create wealth," U.S. Senator David Walsh of Massachusetts told his colleagues. "They transfer wealth."

In the spring of 1922, the United States Senate began debate on a tariff bill, H. R. 7456, an act "to provide revenue, to regulate commerce with foreign countries, to encourage the industries of the United States, and for other purposes." The legislation came to be known as the Fordney-McCumber Act, after its two main Republican sponsors, Representative Joseph Fordney of Michigan, the chair of the House Ways and Means Committee, and Senator Porter McCumber of North Dakota, the chair of the Senate Finance Committee. Senator Walsh had spoken from the well of the Senate many times in opposition to new tariffs.

"The authority to levy taxes upon one group of citizens for the benefit of another group ought to be exercised with the utmost caution," Walsh said. "Surely, nothing less than definite and indisputable facts can justify the exercise of such unusual and arbitrary power."

At the conclusion of World War I, the U.S. economy experienced an economic slump caused by a drop in postwar demand. One of the hardest hit sectors was agriculture, which saw a decline in prices. During the War farmers had borrowed money to expand production to increase exports to meet European demand. But when prices fell after the War, farmers had trouble paying off their loans. There was a domestic surplus of farm products in America and slackening demand in Europe. One of the basic commodities affected by the H.R. 7456 was raw wool.

"In determining the cost of the public of the duties levied in the wool schedule of the Fordney-McCumber tariff bill," Senator Walsh explained to his colleagues, "it is necessary to bear in mind that there are two duties levied which the ultimate consumer must bear. There is, first of all, the cost to the consumer of the duty up on wool--which is levied for the benefit of the wool grower-- and secondly, there is the cost of the protective duties which have been levied for the benefit of the manufacturer. In other words, the purchaser of a woolen blanket, or ready-made dress, or a suit of clothes, or a sweater or any other garment containing wool has had the price which he must pay for his garments and enhanced by law in two particulars."

During his speech on the Senate floor, it was not lost on his colleagues that Walsh was wearing what looked to be a very expensive wool suit. Walsh understood that Republicans in Congress were looking for ways to raise agricultural revenues. One of the political mechanisms available was the tariff, designed to equalize production costs across international markets, and to prevent other countries from dumping products on the market that were below U.S. prices.

The Fordney-McCumber bill would give the President broad powers to raise or lower rates on products by imposing tariffs, with recommendations from the Tariff Commission, a review body created during the Wilson administration. Most Democrats in Congress opposed protectionist tariffs. The Junior Senator from Massachusetts, Mr. Walsh, had become one of the most outspoken opponents of the Fordney-McCumber bill.

"The purchaser of a wool suit must pay a tax to the retailer on every pound of raw wool in the garment, and this tax finds its way back to the wool grower after deductions have been made all along the line by the various middleman. There is another tax which finds its way back to the manufacturer of the woolen cloth. This latter tax is levied on the theory that protects the domestic manufacturer for the difference in the cost of converting wool into cloth here and abroad."

Born in Leominster, Massachusetts, Walsh was the son of Irish Catholic immigrants. He earned his law degree, won a seat in the Massachusetts House of Representatives at the turn of the century, was elected in 1912 as the state's first Democratic Lieutenant Governor in 70 years, and went on to serve as Governor of Massachusetts from 1914 to 1916. He was elected to the U.S. Senate from Massachusetts in 1918, at the age of 46.

Time magazine, which was often merciless to Democrats, described Senator Walsh as a bachelor who was "tall and stout. A double chin tends to get out over his tight-fitting collar. His stomach bulges over his belt. He weighs 200 pounds or more. His dress is dandified. He wears silk shirts in bright colors and stripes and, often, stiff collars to match. His feet are small and well-shod."

"It is impossible," Walsh continued, "to estimate either of these costs with precision, but it is possible to show in a large way what tremendous burdens will be imposed on the consumer by these dual tariff rates levied on wool and woven goods---one for the benefit of the wool grower and the other for the benefit of the manufacturer. The rights of the ultimate consumers have been entirely overlooked. Indeed, the purchasing capacity of the consumer was apparently never considered or discussed by those drafting the bill."

Walsh looked up at his audience. His Democratic friends in the chamber, who numbered around 16, were following his remarks with some amusement, knowing that the Republicans on the other side of the aisle were anxious to see the Senator from Massachusetts sit down. But Walsh did not sit down.

"Let us consider the cost of the raw wool duty to the individual. The increased duties of raw wool and other materials entering into a suit of clothes mean an increase not far from estimated by the clothing trade, which is not less than $4 on the average suit, $7.50 on the average overcoat. On top of all of this there is the protective duty levied for the benefit of the manufacture of dress goods and woolen cloths. With the cheaper dress goods, the spread in price is even greater--that is--the duties are heavier on the clothing of the middle and poor classes."

"Our people are not in a position to bear the increased prices which are bound to follow. Wages have already been reduced and there has been no substantial increase in the salary or income of the salaried man or woman. With a universal demand for a decrease in the cost of production of everything, Congress proceeds to force upward the cost of production. Instead of garments with a reasonable amount of fine wool contained therein, we might expect to see an increase in the class of garments which contain a larger amount cotton or wool shoddies of various kinds."

"That high prices are sure to follow the enactment of the pending tariff bill no one disputes. High prices do not necessarily mean prosperity. High prices have before and may again prove of no benefit to anyone. These exorbitant and excessive rates, in my opinion, will ultimately impoverish the buyer, ruin the seller, and finally deprive labor of employment. These tariffs will amount to a prohibition against wearing woolen clothing."

There was a sustained round of applause from the Democratic side of the aisle as Senator Walsh squared off his papers and left the well. On the Republican side---which controlled the chamber---there was virtual silence---and relief.

Later that afternoon, when Walsh returned from Capitol Hill to his suite of rooms at the Carlton Hotel on 16th Street, the front desk informed the Senator that he had a visitor. A porter brought Walsh over to a thin man in a three-piece suit, with thick eyebrows, wearing glasses and holding an unlit pipe in his left hand.

"Ernst," the man introduced himself. "Attorney Morris Ernst, of Greenbaum, Wolff & Ernst." He handed the Senator his business card

Walsh looked over the card, and looked over the stranger, unsure of his business. "Do I know you?" the Senator asked.

Ernst put his unlit pipe into his left suitcoat pocket. "I listened to your speech today on the Senate floor. More about wool suits than I ever knew," Ernst said, with a smile. "Pretty impressive."

"Thank you," responded Walsh. "There's one common thread to all these tariff debates: the public knows nothing."

"Speaking of a thread," Ernst said. "One of my clients is the *New York Post*. I'm following up on a thread of a story that you may know something about..."

"What story?"

"Do you know a man named Gustave Beekman?"

"No, the name is not familiar to me. Who is this Beekman?"

"He owns--or is a part owner--of an establishment near the Brooklyn Navy Yard on Pacific Street," Ernst said. "A lot of young men in the service are attracted to it."

"Why are you telling me this, Mr. Ernst?"

"Have you no acquaintance with the Pacific street area or Mr. Beekman?" Ernst asked.

"I have not..."

"Have you any acquaintance with a Mr. Virgil Thomson?"

"Mr. Ernst," Walsh said, with some exasperation in his voice, "with due respect, if you are here to lobby me on behalf of some client, please be more to the point. If you kindly will tell me who or what is the object..."

"No, Senator, I am not a legislative agent. My client is the *New York Post*. They asked me to confer with you about Mr. Beekman and the establishment he operates near the Brooklyn Naval Yard."

"Well, as you can see Mr. Ernst, I am at a disadvantage in this conversation, since I know nothing of Mr. Beekman or his business."

"Senator, it's my understanding that you are a bachelor..."

Senator Walsh's face flushed red, and his eyes flashed with impatience. "Where is this interrogation going, Mr. Ernst. I have truly lost the thread of it!"

"Senator, my newspaper is aware that the Federal Bureau of Investigation has been monitoring for some time the activities of this venue in Brooklyn owned by Mr. Beekman. There has been some level of surveillance of the patrons of this establishment."

"What does that have to do with me?"

"Senator, my client, the *New York Post*, believes from evidence, that Mr. Beekman has been running a brothel for homosexuals. They have seen a list of patrons who frequent this location."

"Yes, and..."

"And one of the guests at this club is a prominent musician in some circles. Another is being called 'Senator X' by the paper."

Senator Walsh rose to his feet and stepped closer to Ernst. "And your *client*, Mr. Ernst, has asked you to confirm that I am Senator X?"

"*The New York Post* has no intention to reveal what it knows or doesn't know about this homosexual club. But if you, Senator, have any firsthand knowledge of the operations of Gustave Beekman's club, or have names of people who have visited his club---now would be a good time to disclose what you know, and to cooperate with officials."

"Mr. Ernst," Senator Walsh replied, "I have nothing to tell you for one simple reason: I have never been to this 'club.' I have never spoken to this Beekman, and I am not your Senator X. But this I *can* tell you---if your newspaper ever prints anything about me in connection with this story, I will pursue your newspaper to any length necessary to defend my honor and my reputation from such shoddy muckraking journalism."

Ernst pulled his pipe out of this jacket pocket, felt around in his pants pocket for a match, and then smiled at the Senator.

"That was quite a pretty speech you made today, Senator. A real dandy of a speech, you might say."

Walsh made no reply, locking his eyes straight through Ernst. "You are a madman," Walsh mumbled. "How do I know who you really are?"

Ernst slowly surveyed Walsh from his shoes to his head, taking his time as if to engrave the image in his mind. He paused, and spoke:

"That's a nice suit, Senator. If I'm not mistaken, it's imported tweed wool from the Hebrides, is it not?"

Post Script:

David I. Walsh was the first Irish-Catholic Senator from Massachusetts. Two years after the Fordney-McCumber Act debate, Walsh lost his Senate seat in a tight election. But in 1926, Walsh returned to the Senate to fill out the final two years of the late Massachusetts Senator Henry Cabot Lodge. Walsh served another 18 years in the Senate. At the age of 74, he lost a re-election bid in 1946 to Henry Cabot Lodge, Jr.

Walsh was not a solid supporter of President Franklin Roosevelt, or of the New Deal, but he was the lead sponsor in 1935 of legislation creating a minimum wage and child labor rules for employees of government contractors.

On the floor of the Senate, Walsh spoke out against the Ku Klux Klan and against Nazi Germany and anti-semitism. He was a leading member of the America First movement, and opposed U.S. entry into World War II until the bombing of Pearl Harbor made isolationism almost impossible.

Senator Walsh became entangled in a sex and spy scandal focused on a male brothel for U.S. Navy personnel in Brooklyn, New York that purportedly involved Nazi spies. New York police arrested the brothel's owner, Gustave Beekman, on sodomy charges, along with three foreign agents. Beekman received a 20-year jail sentence.

The New York Post, *which strongly opposed Walsh's position against U.S. involvement in World War II, implicated a "Senator X" in the Brooklyn brothel affair both as a homosexual and a patron of the brothel. The newspaper revealed that Senator X was David Walsh and suggested that Walsh was a tool of enemy agents.*

Walsh called The Post's *tabloid-style story "a diabolical lie." An investigation by the FBI failed to produce any connection between the brothel and Senator Walsh. Although the FBI report was not entered into the Congressional Record, the Senate Majority Leader concluded that there was no record of Senator Walsh visiting a "house of degradation," and declared that Walsh's reputation was "unsullied." The New York Post called the FBI report a "whitewash for Walsh."*

After leaving the Senate, Walsh returned to Central Massachusetts, where he died in the summer of 1947, at the age of 75.

Morris Ernst was an attorney in New York City. He co-founded the law firm of Greenbaum, Wolff & Ernst in 1915. Two years later he helped organize the National Civil Liberties Bureau, which was the precursor to the American Civil Liberties Union.

Ernst went to court in the 1930s to defend the novel Ulysses against obscenity charges. In the 1940s he barred communists from working at the

ACLU. In 1952, he wrote a book called Report on the American Communist, which profiled 300 former communists, and explained why they renounced communism.

Ernst was politically close to President Franklin Roosevelt and Harry Truman. A Senator from Missouri charged that Morris Ernst had sought a meeting with FDR in the White House to try to smear Senator David Walsh's career because he was against America joining the War.

Morris Ernst died In New York City in 1976 at the age of 88.

ALBERT NORMAN

Albert Norman is an author and activist. For more than 30 years he has been a lobbyist in the Massachusetts General Court focused on the rights of Older Americans.

A former journalist for *Newsweek* magazine, Norman has a Master's Degree in Comparative Literature from Columbia University, and a Masters in Teaching from the University of Massachusetts.

For 25 years, Norman has worked with citizen's groups to stop unwanted commercial developments. Norman's first book, *Slam Dunking Wal-Mart: How You Can Stop Superstore Sprawl* (Raphel, 1999), has become an underground classic for neighborhood groups, and his second book, *The Case Against Wal-Mart* was released in June of 2004. Both books have been translated into Japanese. His latest book, *Occupy Walmart* (Brigantine Media) was published in May of 2012. This book is a collection of essays published while he was a contributor to *The Huffington Post*.

Norman is the founder of Sprawl-Busters, an international clearinghouse on big box sprawl, who has guided hundreds of communities around the world fighting corporations like Wal-Mart.

In September of 2004, *Forbes* magazine called Norman "Wal-Mart's #1 Enemy." He first stopped a Wal-Mart in his hometown of Greenfield in 1993. Norman was featured in the PBS documentary *Store Wars*, about one Virginia town's battle against Wal-Mart; in the 2003 ITVS film *Talking to the Wall;* served as a consultant for the movie *High Cost of Low Price"* in 2005; was featured in the *Our Town* movie in Damariscotta, Maine in 2006, and in the Canadian movie *Wal-Mart Nation* in 2007. In 2007 Al appeared on Penn & Teller's show *Bullshit*.

Norman has traveled throughout America, Canada, Mexico, Japan, Ireland, Puerto Rico, and Barbados at the request of citizen's groups and small businesses.

Albert Norman's work has been covered extensively by the media. In February, 2001, the *London Sunday Times Magazine* called Norman a "fire-breathing evangelist". His appearance on *60 Minutes* in 1995 earned him the title "guru of the anti-Wal-Mart movement." "He's been invited to preach the anti-Wal-Mart gospel in dozens of towns," said *60 Minutes*. The *Wall Street Journal* has called Norman "a one-man anti-Wal-Mart cottage industry." Norman's work was featured in journalist Bob Ortega's book *In Sam We Trust*; in Jim Hightower's book *Thieves in High Places*; in the book *How Superstore Sprawl is Harming Communities* by the National Trust for Historic Preservation, and in former Sierra Club President Adam Werbach's book, *Act Now, Apologize Later*.

Albert Norman has appeared on the *Lehrer News Hour, NBC Nightly News, ABC's Nightline, The Wall Street Journal Report, CNBC Steals & Deals, Marketplace, The Al Franken Show, Talk of the Nation*, NPR's *Here & Now*, NPR's *Morning Edition, The Osgood File*, The Atlantic Magazine, and has been written up in *The Boston Globe, Time Magazine, and hundreds of small town daily newspapers.* In 1994 he wrote *Eight Ways to Stop the Store* in *The Nation* magazine, which was reprinted in *The Utne Reader*.

Norman lives in Western Massachusetts.

Contacts:

www.sprawl-busters.com

413-834-4284

21 Grinnell St. Greenfield, MA 01301

Book Link: http://www.sprawl-busters.com/occupywalmart.html